DEATH GROUND

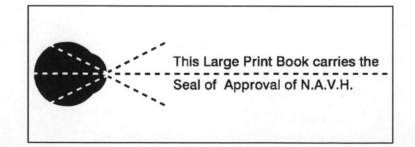

This Large Print Book carries the
Seal of Approval of N.A.V.H.

DEATH GROUND

ED GORMAN

THORNDIKE PRESS
A part of Gale, Cengage Learning

Detroit • New York • San Francisco • New Haven, Conn • Waterville, Maine • London

GALE
CENGAGE Learning™

Copyright © 1988 by Edward Gorman.
Thorndike Press, a part of Gale, Cengage Learning.

LIBRARY OF CONGRESS CATALOGING-IN-PUBLICATION DATA

Gorman, Edward.
    Death ground / by Ed Gorman. — Large print ed.
      p. cm. — (Thorndike Press large print romance)
    ISBN-13: 978-1-4104-2691-8
    ISBN-10: 1-4104-2691-2
    1. Large type books. I. Title.
    PS3557.O759.D4 2010
    813'.54—dc22
                                 2010019728

Published in 2010 by arrangement with Leisure Books, a division of Dorchester Publishing Co., Inc.

Printed in the United States of America
1 2 3 4 5 6 7 14 13 12 11 10

To Sara Ann Freed,
my good and gentle phone friend.

I would like to thank Tom Owens
for his help with my books.

CHAPTER ONE

You could tell it was a well-kept house. On the way up the stairs with the straw-haired girl in the gingham dress and the high-button shoes one size too big, Leo Guild had to step aside to let an Indian woman toting a bucket of soapy water pass by him. She carried a mop and had a forehead shiny with sweat, and she sure looked as if she knew how to keep things clean. If the girls took equal care of themselves, Guild tonight would have himself a pleasant if slightly lonely birthday. He was fifty-four today.

The girl said, half an hour later, "I bet you're mad."

Guild said nothing.

"I bet you wish you woulda picked one of the other girls, don't ya?"

Guild still said nothing.

"I can't help it. Sometimes I just can't do it. Sometimes I get to thinkin' about all the things the preacher used to say, and then I just can't do it. I just can't." She paused. "It's nothin' personal. I mean, you don't offend me or nothin'."

"Gosh, thanks."

"You just got a kind face. I figgered you'd understand. Some men do and —"

"— and some men don't."

The girl got flustered and looked scared.

In the small room with the too-soft bed and the melancholy shadows of kerosene light, Guild laughed somewhat sadly. "I guess it's just the way luck's been running."

"Bad luck, huh?"

"Tracked a man six hundred miles through the snow and damn near lost a finger to frostbite, and the day before I caught up with him and the two-thousand-dollar reward I would have gotten, he dropped dead of a heart attack."

"Gol."

"Then I signed on as a stagecoach guard and before I reached the first stage stop, the company went bankrupt."

"Cripes."

He looked her over in the lamp glow. She hadn't taken her clothes off. She looked like a farm girl dressed up for a Saturday night with a farm boy. His body wanted her, but his soul didn't because her soul didn't want him. He never liked it in the houses, but he was fifty-four and in many ways he had lived too much and in many ways he had lived too little, and even though he couldn't talk about too much or too little with anybody, he could hold somebody in the darkness, and the mere fact of holding them would be enough to get him through this night of fifty-four years.

But the girl, too skinny and plain to ever be particularly profitable for a house like this, did not want to hold him, so now he took the rye from the bedstand and the cigarette he'd rolled earlier in the day and he had his own little celebration.

"You mad?"

"Nope." He smoked his cigarette.

"You gonna tell Patty?"

"Nope." He drank his rye.

"You gonna hit me?"

"Nope." He stared into the deep shadows of the room and listened to the cold October night rattle the window. Then he thought of the little girl. Sometimes it happened like that. Suddenly she was there in his mind, and so was what he'd done.

"You look sad, mister."

"Old is all."

"Fifty-four ain't old."

"Some fifty-fours ain't old. Mine is."

He was already up and straightening his clothes, the black suit coat and white boiled shirt and gray serge trousers and black Texas boots. He eased the black Stetson onto his gray hair. Finally he tugged the holster holding his .44 around his waist and into proper place.

She glanced up at him with her quick kid face. "You sure ain't gonna tell Patty?"

He leaned over and kissed her on the forehead. "I'm not going to tell Patty."

He left the money on the battered bureau, and then he ducked his six feet under the door frame and went on downstairs.

Several men sat anxiously in the parlor, waiting. They might have been at a train depot waiting for some big black engine to take them someplace fantastic. They looked that excited.

Patty, the woman who ran the place, came up and said, "She good?"

"Real good."

She poked him in the ribs and grinned. She had food in her teeth. "All my girls are good."

He went to the door, and on the way out she said to his back, "All of them."

He was ten steps down the sidewalk, dead leaves scraping the boards of the walk, the silver alien moon full and ominous in the cloudless sky, when he saw a short man in a three-piece suit carrying a Winchester hurrying toward him.

The man, breathlessly, said, "You Guild?"

Guild nodded.

"I'm Deputy Forbes."

"Glad to meet you."

"Sheriff wants to see you."

"He say why?"

"He said why, but he also said I wasn't supposed to say why."

Guild, expansive on the rye, said, "He say why you weren't supposed to say why?"

"Your cheeks cold?"

"No, but my nose is."

"Good," Deputy Forbes said. "Then let's go back to the office and we can discuss this in a nice warm place." Then he raised his young, pudgy face to the fancy house whose light faltered in the prairie shadows behind. "She's got some good girls in there, that Patty does."

"Yes," Guild said, "that's what I heard."

CHAPTER TWO

Decker was typical of the kind of law you saw in the Territory these days. The old kind, the gunfighters who'd roamed town to town taking a piece of prostitution and gambling and liquor, were gone. Just this summer four of them had been hanged in Yankton. The territorial governor had called it "a symbol of our new dedication to law and order." Such statements always made Guild smile. If it was your neck in the noose, it was a lot more than symbolic.

Decker stood maybe five-eight and weighed maybe one-forty. He had a handsome but unremarkable face and wore eyeglasses. His brown hair was thinning and he wore a three-piece brown suit on the right lapel of which rested the smallest three-pointed star Guild had ever seen. He looked like a banker who might get tough with you after a few beers.

His office continued the impression that

he was a businessman. Behind a wide mahogany desk was a glass-paneled book-case with enough law tomes to make a young lawyer envious. On the desk itself was a tinytype of Decker, a pretty plump woman, and two pretty plump little girls. To the right of the desk was a long glass case filled with rifles and shotguns. The floor had a gray hooked rug. On a small service table to the left of the desk was a nickel-plated coffeepot from which Decker poured Guild a cup without asking.

Guild thanked him for it and sat down.

"Across the alley is the back door of the undertaker's," Decker said.

"I see."

"We put two men in there about an hour ago."

Guild sipped his coffee. He knew what was coming.

"One of them was Merle Rig. He a good friend of yours?" Decker said.

"Actually, he was sort of an enemy."

Decker put down his tin cup and seemed to give Guild a reassessment, as if Guild had been hiding something only now re-vealed.

"Kind of funny you would be a bodyguard for a man you consider an enemy."

"He paid me."

13

"Still."

"Winter's coming and I'm fifty-four and I don't have much money. He paid me two hundred dollars."

"Why was he your enemy?"

Guild shrugged. "Ten years ago we were doing some bounty hunting together. The day we were to collect, he knocked me out and went in and got the reward for himself."

"But you agreed to be his bodyguard anyway?"

"I was passing through town here and he heard about it and he came to me and said that somebody was after him. He said he'd been sick the last week or so and couldn't defend himself and would I watch him."

"Ever wonder why he didn't come to me for protection?"

"Didn't have to wonder. I assumed he was in trouble the law could only make worse." '

"You lived in a nice world, Mr. Guild."

"It's the only one that'll have me," Guild said, thinking about the little girl again and how people reacted once they knew who he was and what he'd done.

"A month ago he robbed the local bank here of fifteen thousand dollars," Decker said. "He and a mountain man named Kriker."

"The hell."

14

"I'm sure it was Kriker who came into town and killed him and the kid." He paused, following Guild's eyes to the certificate on the wall. These days in the Territory, lawmen went to one of the territorial capitals where they taught courses in being a lawman. Decker said, "The kid has a mother here. You shouldn't have gotten him involved."

"I'm sorry I did, but he wanted to. He said he wanted to be a deputy but you wouldn't let him."

"He was too raw. He had a head full of fancy notions that wouldn't do this office or himself a damn bit of good."

"He wasn't a bad bodyguard. He stayed sober and he was punctual and he was reasonably good with a Remington. That's why he was there tonight. Spelling me."

"He was back shot."

Guild sighed. "You talk to his mother?"

"That's a privilege I'm going to give you, Mr. Guild. Technically, you were his employer. Seems to me it would only be fitting."

Guild finished his coffee and set the tin cup carefully on the fine shiny wood of the desk. Decker pushed a round leather coaster over to him. Decker was exactly the sort of man who would use coasters.

15

Decker said, "Tomorrow two of my deputies are going after Kriker. You have any interest in joining them?"

"Thought I'd just be moving on."

"They're young and they could use help."

"You could always go."

"I could if I didn't have to testify in a very important case tomorrow morning in the next county."

"I see."

"It's time we got Kriker. You know him?"

"No."

"Has his own little encampment up in the sand hills. Suspected him of a lot of things over the years but was never able to prove anything. There's a thousand-dollar reward for the money and the men who robbed the bank."

"What makes you think you can prove anything now?"

"Day of the robbery the dead man and Kriker were seen together in a local saloon. Plus I've got a strong suspicion that we'll find the money somewhere in Kriker's encampment."

"Why would Kriker kill him?"

"He was weakening, your friend. Or enemy. Or whatever the hell he was. He sent me a note."

"A note?"

"Yes."

"When did you get it?"

"Just this afternoon."

"Funny he didn't mention anything to me about a note."

Decker made a face that said a lot funnier things had happened.

"You mind if I see the note?" Guild said.

Decker opened a drawer and took out a long white envelope and opened the flap. From inside the envelope he took a piece of gray paper that had been folded several times. He handed it across the desk to Guild. The paper was cheap and smudgy. In a broad shaky hand were written the words: *I'd like to talk to you about me and Kriker's part in the First Citizen Bank robbery.* It was signed *Merle Rig.*

Guild frowned.

"Something wrong, Mr. Guild?"

"Far as I knew, Merle Rig couldn't either read or write."

"Maybe he had somebody write it for him."

"Maybe."

Decker took the note back and put it in the envelope and put the envelope in the drawer and then put his social face on again, the one he wore in the tinytype with the plump Decker brood.

17

Decker said, "I need you to go across the alley with me. All right, Mr. Guild?"

There were two of them and they were naked. They lay on tables in a back room noisy with the banging of creaky shutters caught in a Halloween wind. Blood soaked the sheets that covered them.

He looked at the kid first and nodded, and then he looked at Merle Rig and nodded. Rig had nickels covering his eyes. Pennies stained green.

The undertaker, a stout man with the flushed cheeks and bloodstained apron of a good German butcher, started to draw the sheet back over Merle Rig's face, but Guild stopped him.

Guild wanted to stare at the face a moment longer. He wasn't sure shy. They hadn't been so different, not in the final tally of things, Rig and Guild. Rig made one kind of mistake and Guild another, and that was about all. He stood there and thought how he should have told Rig that he didn't give a particular damn about Rig knocking him out and taking the reward all for himself. People were just people and sometimes they did terrible things. Everybody did.

The Halloween wind came. The guttering

kerosene lamps in the death room fluttered and cast long cavelike shadows.

Decker said, "I don't know about you, Mr. Guild, but it's real easy to get tired of staring at dead people. How about letting him draw the sheet back up?"

Guild looked up at the undertaker, who was wiping his bloody hands off on his apron.

Guild nodded and the undertaker drew the sheet back over Merle Rig.

Decker put a piece of paper in Guild's hand. "Here's where the kid's mother lives."

"You don't think this is your job?"

Decker said, "I wasn't stupid enough to hire him."

CHAPTER THREE

The woman lived in a boardinghouse that smelled of laundry soap and cabbage and pipe tobacco. She lived in a wide room built off the east end of the two-story frame house. He went up two steps and started to knock and then he looked through the glass and past the curtain to where the lamplight was like butter and where she sat in cheap calico and a shawl, darning a pair of gray work socks. She was old not so much in years, but worn-out old. When he did knock finally and she looked up finally, he saw that in fact she was not older than forty and that buried in the rawboned face were beautiful blue eyes.

She got up and came to the door and said, "Help you, mister?"

"You'd be Kenny's mother."

She knew right away something was wrong. She crossed herself. "My God."

Guild said, "I'd like to come in."

"You're that man who hired him, ain't you?"

"Please," he said, taking off his hat and nodding to the interior.

There was a daybed covered now with a quilt and throw pillows so it would resemble a couch. Against the opposite wall was a bed. The furniture consisted of a rocking chair and a kitchen table and a cupboard and a stove. The air smelled of cinnamon. Guild thought of his own mother and his boyhood on a farm when even in the best of times you got twenty-five cents for wheat and two cents a pound for dressed pork.

She put a hand on his wrist and said, "He's dead, ain't he?"

"Yes."

"My God."

"I'm sorry, ma'am."

"You there?"

"When it happened?" Guild asked.

"Yup."

"No. No, I wasn't there."

"Where was you?"

He thought of the fancy house and the farm girl who hadn't wanted to. "I had business. Tonight's my birthday." He thought maybe the last remark would buy him a little sympathy. Then he was ashamed of himself. Her son was dead. She should be

21

the one seeking sympathy, not him.

She backed into the room. She had the dazed look that often accompanies news of death. In Guild's experience people tended to do one of two things: just kind of float and fade the way she was, or get angry. She floated over to the daybed and sat down, so light the springs didn't squeak at all, and folded her old-woman hands one across the other in her lap and then looked up at him with her young-woman eyes.

She began sobbing then, and he just stood there and listened to her. She swore and she prayed and then she did them both again.

Finally he went over through the cinnamon-smelling air in the butter-gold light of the little room and sat on the bed. This time the springs did squeak and he put his big arm around her and sort of tucked her inside him, and then, as he knew she would, she just cried all the more.

They sat there for a very long time like this beneath the cheap print of a very sad Jesus. Knowing what Jesus knew, Guild had good reason to be sad.

"He nearly died soon as they took him from my womb." She looked over at him. "His lungs, the doc said. Never did have good lungs."

Guild nodded.

This was half an hour later.

She had insisted on fixing them tea. It was cinnamon tea. The wind rattled the windows.

She said, "You hear him cough?"

"Yes."

"Never did have good lungs."

She was crazed, repeating herself. The least he could do was sit there and listen and drink her cinnamon tea.

"He wanted to be a sheriff."

"That's what he told me."

"Wouldn't have made a good one, though. Too skittish."

"Oh."

"Our whole family's skittish."

Guild didn't know what to say. He felt unable to move, unable to speak. He just sat there. There were three of them in the room. Her and Guild and the dead son, Kenny.

"His pa was skittish, too. Died in the mines, his pa did."

"I'm sorry."

"Kenny was all I had." She started crying again. "He never should have started hanging around that Bruckner."

"Bruckner?"

"One of the sheriff's deputies. He was always doin' little favors for Bruckner and his brother James, and they was always fill-in' his head with the idea that he was gonna be a deputy someday." She looked at him and her grief made him glance away, ashamed. "You filled his head, too."

"He came to me, ma'am."

"But you should've known better."

He sighed. "Now that I think about it, yes, I think I should have."

"They offered him twenty-seven cents an hour to work over to the wagonworks, and he turned it down just so's he could be a bodyguard to that Rig fella. Rig wasn't no good."

Guild was surprised by the familiarity in her voice. "You knew Rig?"

"Sure. He come here several times."

"Rig came here? When?"

"About a month and a half ago."

When Guild hired him, Kenny Tolliver had been careful to pretend that he didn't know Rig at all. Guild said, "So they knew each other pretty well?"

"Kenny, he came home drunk several nights and said he'd been with them."

"Them?"

"Sure. Rig and Bruckner and James."

"The deputies and Rig knew each other?"

"Sure." She looked at him more carefully now.

"Something wrong?"

"Don't know yet, I guess."

She said, "You work six months at the wagon-works, they give you a raise."

"It sounds like a decent job."

"I know a fellow making thirty-nine cents an hour there. Been there fourteen years."

"I'm sorry, Mrs. Tolliver." Then: "He never mention a man named Kriker?"

"Kriker? No, not that I recollect."

He stood up. He made a very elaborate thing out of putting his hat on and fixing it just so on his head. She sat once more in the buttery light with her old body and young eyes and watched him.

"You never should have hired him," she said.

She was crying once more.

"No," he said. "No, Mrs. Tolliver, I shouldn't have."

CHAPTER FOUR

He got up at 4:00 A.M. Even then, he had to hurry. There was a lot to do.

He went down the rooming house hallway to the pump and filled his pitcher and then went back to the commode basin and washed himself very well. It might be days before he got a chance to clean himself this well again. He even washed behind his ears the way his older sister had always told him to. She was dead now from consumption, and so the memory was bittersweet.

In his saddlebags he'd been carrying a brand-new red union suit from Sears he hadn't gotten around to wearing. He put the long johns on this morning and then his regular clothes and then he gathered up everything, including the rifle he intended to trade and his .44 and his sheepskin.

Dawn was a pinkish streak behind the peaks and turrets of the town's fancier houses. The wagon tracks in the streets were frozen solid. Guild's breath was a pure white plume. His nose was cold and he was glad he'd used the hemmorhoid salve a doc had given him. Chill temperatures and saddle leather got tough on you.

The first stop was a Catholic church. A plump priest was saying an early mass for immigrant women and a few male workers. The church was crude, wood instead of the marble you saw in the big Territory towns, but the stations of the cross had been rendered in Indian art, probably Sioux, and were interesting to look at. The smell of incense was very sweet and he enjoyed hearing the small choir chant in Latin. Even though he had no idea what the words meant, they carried dignity and reassurance.

He sat in the last pew, in the shadows, and he did not kneel when the rest of them knelt, and he did not rise for communion when the rest of them rose. He kept staring at the stations of the cross. In them Christ had slightly Indian features.

Then mass ended and he got up and walked up the center aisle to the altar and called out for the priest, who was skinny and bald and had a wart on his cheek. The two Indian altar boys watched Guild curiously. To the priest, Guild said, "I would like you to hear my confession, Father." The priest nodded and waved the two altar boys away.

The priest looked around and said, "The church is empty. We can do it right here."

"That would be fine."

"You look troubled."

"I am troubled."

The priest in his silk vestments pointed to a corner over by the votive candles. There were two chairs there. The priest said, "Why don't we sit down?"

"I've never made a confession sitting down."

The priest smiled. "Tradition isn't everything."

So they went over and sat down and Guild said, "Forgive me, Father, for I have sinned. It has been three months since my last confession."

"All right, my son. What weighs on you?"

"A little girl," Guild said. Ordinarily he followed the usual form for making a confession, starting with the lesser sins first and leading up to the more important ones. But he decided that since they had already broken formality by sitting down, he might as well break formality by talking only about one thing. "I killed a little girl."

The priest had to pretend not to be shocked, but of course he was shocked. You could not hear about killing little girls and not be shocked.

"You did this on purpose?"

"No."

The priest looked enormously relieved. "Then why do you confess it?"

So Guild told him, as Guild always did whenever the dreams of the little girl got particularly bad again, as they had been lately. Guild was not even Catholic. It was simply that confession, unlike whiskey, seemed to help the dreams. At least temporarily.

The second stop was at the livery stable. The liveryman had furry white muttonchops and wore a Prince Albert suit and a homburg. He obviously wanted to be seen as a prosperous merchant. The right hand he put forth for Guild to shake sparkled with diamonds. He had a Negro to do the real work, cleaning up the manure, grooming the animals, gentling them out back in a rope corral.

What lay ahead required a better animal than the grulla he'd come into town on.

The liveryman showed him several animals. When Guild saw the shave-tailed Appaloosa, he thought about the time he'd served a three-day sentence for assault and battery. He'd seen a drunken wrangler showing off for friends by trying to break a particularly troublesome stallion. Finally the wrangler got so humiliated that he took out a knife and slashed the stallion's throat. Guild had gone over and kicked in three of the man's ribs and broken his nose. He had one of those tempers.

He looked at the Appaloosa and said, "How much?"

"Too cold to dicker," the liveryman said, patting his hands together.

They made a deal.

By now the town of false fronts and two-story brick buildings was well awake. The sky was low and gray and wintry. The trees were naked and the grass was brown and you could smell serious snow coming. In the distance the mountains showed snow on their caps. Below this were the sand hills where the man named Kriker resided. Guild ate three eggs and sausage and slice browns in a restaurant filled with angry talk about the Territory's latest political crisis — the notion that the Territory could force your child to go to school for five years, whether you needed that child as a farmhand or not. At least in this restaurant, the idea was not a popular one.

The woman at the general store was fifty but very attractive in a gingham dress and spectacles with gold rims. She put Guild in mind of women who made good cherry pies and knew when, as lovers, to be ferocious and when, the night suddenly oppressive with a man's memories, to be gentle.

But there were other things to be done than spark a lady, and Guild wasn't all that comfortable in the sparking department anyway.

She showed him ten weapons and he held them all and sighted them and held them some more. Finally he asked her how much she'd give him in trade for the Remington and so they concluded their deal.

He walked out of there with a double 10-gauge.

Now he was ready. He had thought about how Rig had been killed, and he had thought about how young Kenny Tolliver had been killed, and he had thought about how they'd both known the deputies, and he had thought about how the bank had been held up, and he had thought about the man named Kriker.

None of it seemed to make sense, of course, but then when he thought about it, it all made a great deal of sense.

He figured he owed Rig a death. Maybe

he even owed the Tolliver kid a death, and so he hefted his new-bought double 10-gauge.

CHAPTER FIVE

The first deputy, Thomas Bruckner, turned out to be a tall man in a beaver coat and a fedora and a brilliant blue glass eye, the other one being all right. He also had a gold tooth and an almost constant grin short on mirth and long on malice. When Guild walked into Sheriff Decker's office, Thomas Bruckner looked at his partner, his brother James Bruckner, and winked.

Guild recognized the wink.

He had seen it many times over the past four years, ever since the trial.

It meant that the man winking and the other man grinning in response knew all about Guild.

Or thought they did, anyway.

James was an awkward man in a greasy duster and several layers of clothes beneath. His knuckles had been busted so many times they sat on his hands like ornaments. But that wasn't what you really noticed about James Bruckner. No, what you really noticed was how the left side of his face had an unnatural, leathery look, the result of burns that must have occurred in childhood. The stretched texture of the skin looked as if the scars did not quite want to cover the man's face.

Sheriff Decker and the kid deputy Forbes were behind Decker's desk, going over papers.

Guild said, "I'm going with these two for Kriker."

The grins faded fast and Decker's head came up.

"Morning, Mr. Guild." He had changed suits. He wore a western-cut number this morning, but it was tweed and it was immaculate and he still looked more merchant than lawman. He looked neither distressed nor surprised, though certainly the Bruckners did. "What changed your mind?"

Guild decided to make things simple. No reasons to share his suspicions. He said, "You said there was a thousand-dollar reward for return of the money."

"Indeed."

"Well, that's why I'm going."

The room smelled of coffee and cigar smoke. Outside in the hall ragged prisoners were being pushed out of the door on the way to court appearances at the county courthouse down the street. One of them glanced in at the men in the office and gathered a great wad of white spit and sent it flying into the room.

Thomas Bruckner lifted his Sharps and pointed it at the man. "Give me a double eagle if I can hit him in the balls?"

James laughed.

A deputy pushed the prisoner out of the way.

Then the Bruckners turned back to Decker.

Thomas Bruckner said, "Won't ride with him, Sheriff."

This time Decker did look surprised. "Why not? Said you wouldn't mind an extra man."

"You know what you found out over the telegraph," Thomas said, " 'bout the little girl and all."

"He was acquitted," Decker said.

"Still and all," Thomas said.

Guild said, "Makes no never-mind to me, Sheriff. If they want an extra man, I'll go along with them. If not, I'll find this Kriker on my own."

Thomas grinned his hateful grin. "Bounty man. Lots of confidence. You ever been in the sand hills in this weather, bounty man?"

"So happens I have."

Thomas said, "You ever stalked a man so crazy even the goddamn Indians are scared of him?"

Guild nodded to Decker. "I'll be going now, Sheriff. Just thought you'd like to know my intentions."

The Bruckners glanced at each other and then Thomas said to Guild, "Thought you were goin' with us."

"Thought you didn't ride with a man like me."

Another glance. Guild could guess what they were thinking: He would be easier to control if he were with them.

"You're all right," Thomas said. "Just kind of testin' your mettle a little."

Guild said, "I wouldn't do that real often if I were you."

Thomas laughed. "You got a lot of pride for a bounty man. Especially for a bounty man who killed a little girl."

James said, touching his burned skin, "Ease off on him, Thomas. Ease off on him."

For a moment Guild and James stared at each other. They had something in common — James, his burned face; Guild, the dead girl. It made them outcasts; it made them prey.

Thomas glared at his brother and then

yanked on his sleeve. "Come on, we'll go get ready so we can meet the bounty man here in half an hour."

He tilted his hat to the Sheriff and then jerked his brother through the door. Obviously he didn't like the idea of his brother telling him to "ease off" anybody.

When the Bruckners went to get ready, Guild said to Decker, "Strange company for a man like you."

"Meaning?"

"Meaning I doubt they went up to Yankton and took one of those courses on law."

Deputy Forbes smiled his kid smile. Obviously he had gone to Yankton.

Decker pushed a tin cup of coffee Guild's way, stuck a pipe in his mouth, and said, "Territory's changing, but it hasn't changed completely yet. We've got telegraph and a few telephones and transcontinental railroads, but we still have need of men like the Bruckners."

"You trust them?"

Decker's smile, so friendly, was quick. "About as much as I trust you, Mr. Guild. About as much as I trust you."

CHAPTER SIX

Kriker pushed back the burlap curtain and came into the small room inside the soddie that was veined with buffalo grass thick as a man's arm and that generally stayed cool in summer and warm in winter. At noon on the overcast day, the shadows were deep and the moisture-swollen walls cold to touch.

The girl lay on a cot beneath a pile of buffalo hides lively with ticks and other vermin. The girl was eight or nine; Kriker had never been sure. Even from here he could see that she was not better. She was worse.

Kneeling next to her was a raw, angular old woman dressed in a manlike getup of different kinds of hide that she'd cured herself and wore year round. Even by standards of this settlement, the old woman smelled, and even the men who worked the kill told jokes about her.

She raised her gray head to Kriker. She was angry. "You got to give it time to work."

Kriker was a chunky man but not fat. He shaved no oftener than every few weeks and wore a buckskin jacket and a buckskin hat. He carried two .44s stuck into a wide belt and a knife with which he'd cut out the innards of squirrels for dinner. Of course he cut other things with it, too. He said he was in his fortieth summer but no one, especially Kriker, could be sure of this.

He was known throughout the Territory as a man who had robbed banks, trains, and wealthy homes, and who had shot, stabbed, and drowned any number of people who he felt were in need of such fates. He was known in the settlement as the man who'd bitten off the Mountie's nose, this being up near the territorial border where a young and overzealous Mountie had tried to arrest Kriker for something he hadn't done. Kriker calmly presented his side of the case, but still the mountie wanted to take him in. Kriker threw the man to the ground and there ensued a terrible wrestling match, the Mountie having won his post wrestling title many times, and finally Kriker resorted to something he'd heard mountain men talk about but had never seen done. He clamped his teeth on to the Mountie's nose and bit down hard as he could. It was no easy task to tear off a man's nose. But that afternoon

Harry Kriker did exactly that. After three minutes or so, all that was left of the Mountie's nose was a red, running hole. Kriker returned to the encampment. Three other encampment men had been with him. They never tired telling the story, and encampment people never tired of hearing it.

But that sort of frivolity was long past Kriker now as he stood staring down at the frail blond girl with the sweaty face and death-shut eyes.

Kriker moved closer to the girl. Looked at her carefully.

He reached down and put his hand beneath the buffalo robes and took her wrist, frail as a flower stem, and felt for a pulse. Faintly, he felt one.

"You do what you said you was goin' to?" he said to the granny woman.

The woman was nervous now. At one time Kriker had had a wife and son, the story went, and they took sick from milk that had not been put far enough down the well for keeping. A doc was brought from the closest town. Kriker's wife and son died anyway. That night the doc was found on the stage trail back to town. His eyes had been dug out with just the sort of knife you'd cut up squirrels with. A sheriff had come out and there had been an investigation and all of the local newspapers had run angry editorials about Harry Kriker and all the things he had been suspected of over the years, but as usual Kriker and the encampment went on. The doc was buried with a mask over his eyes.

Obviously the granny woman thought of the doc now as she rose, her old knees cracking, and said, "I give her the rattlesnake."

"The heart?"

"The heart."

"And nothin' more?"

"And nothin' more."

"Then why the hell's she still sick? You said it would work."

Her worn brown eyes grew evasive. "I said it might take a day or two."

All his life Kriker had trusted granny women. He had been raised in the hills, and in the hills you did not trust docs because when you did your wife and your son died. But granny women knew things docs didn't know at all. How to get rid of birthmarks by rubbing the marks for three days against the hand of a newly dead corpse; how to get rid of whooping cough by putting the cougher's neck through a horse collar three times; and how to cure bedwetting — this as a last resort if beating the child didn't

41

work — by feeding the child the hind legs of a rat fried just so.

Granny women knew all about these things.

Yet this granny woman, Sadra, had been working with the girl now three days and the girl was only getting worse.

Sadra said, "It ain't like she's your kin."

Kriker raised angry eyes to her. Nobody in the settlement understood. Three years ago he'd held up a stage and the men he'd been with had been too full of fear to go gentle. Driver and passengers had all been killed — except for the girl. They'd wanted to kill her, too, but Kriker had said, no, he would take her back to the encampment. The girl had become his life. When in town he bought her dresses. When in the timber he cut her rattlesnakes and gave her their rattle as toys. He fed her, he sang to her mountain songs in his sure strong voice, and he cradled her when she became afraid of the lightning and thunder of summer storms.

Yet never once in the three years had the girl said a word. He saw in the blue of her eyes that her life had stopped somehow when she'd seen her parents shot to death on the stage road that day, and that no pretty dress or gentle mountain song could ease those blue eyes.

And so he simply revered her.

He slept on a hide cot next to her, and he brought her her meals, and on a day he designated as a birthday he brought her something new and shiny from town.

But she never thanked him, of course. She just sat huddled in the corner of the soddie and watched him, though mostly she seemed to be looking at something no one but she could see.

He told her of the flowers and how they smelled and how you could hold them like infants; and he told her of the mountain streams and how pure and cold the water was; and he told her of how animals could be more loyal and trustworthy friends than human beings ever could, and that was why there was no pleasure in killing animals but sometimes there was pleasure in killing human beings.

He told her all of these things many times — this big hairy shaggy man that judges all over the Territory were just waiting to hang — told her in the soft voice he used to use with his wife and son . . . and she didn't hear.

Or didn't seem to, anyway.

And now she lay ill and he feared the worst and his voice grew threatening with the granny woman.

He stood up. "I got to go see the priest." He nodded to the bed. "You take care of this girl, hear? I want her up on her feet before tomorrow."

He leaned down and kissed the girl on the forehead.

"You hear me, granny woman?"

The threat was clear.

The granny woman nodded and he left.

If you stood on one of the smaller sand hills and looked into the valley below, you saw it, the settlement of sixteen soddies, with a cleared common square for meetings and children. To the east, near the stream, was where the slaughtering was done, usually by the men. The cows were knocked out and then stabbed though the breast and then bled, this blood becoming blood meal for fertilizer. Then each carcass was cut in half, right down the spine, then into quarters. Tanners in town bought the hides, with hooves and horns going to the glue factory. Even the offal was used, for tankage. This was men's work, of course.

The women did not want to do this kind of work, but it was about the only kind of work they did not do. They did candle making, knitting, weaving, soapmaking, spinning, herding, milking, wood carrying, planting, and harvesting (there was a woman named Beulah who could drive a team of ten oxen). The married women bore children and the young girls stockpiled clothes and skills as part of their trousseaus. A woman who could do heavy fieldwork, for example, was looked on just as fondly as a beauty.

This then was the settlement, and it had been this settlement for ten years now, ever since Kriker had first come here on the run from a shoot-out in Montana. He had cleared the trees and made his peace with those Indians who had yet to drift to the drab reservations constructed by the Yankees. He had also invited the rabble who made up the settlement, "rabble" because the first generation here was much like Kriker himself: thieves and counterfeiters and arsonists and killers. They had come to escape prison or the treachery of streets in Chicago or St. Loo or Toronto.

They had come because Kriker had told them that they could establish a settlement and raise everything they needed to feed and clothe themselves, and it had been a wonderful ringing dream delivered in Kriker's pulpitlike oratory. So they had come, in rags and tatters, men of rage and

45

melancholy, women without virtues or loyalty, and even though at first many of them deserted, returning to the familiar filth of the cities, enough of them stayed that the settlement prospered and those who stayed were transformed from rubble into human beings with purpose and dignity. The first corn came up and blackbirds had to be chased off; wild strawberries were picked in June and grain yellow as gold was toted in smoky September; and the women, the tireless ceaseless women, found that butter and eggs fetched good prices for a mere day's buckboard ride into town.

The settlement was born and grew and prospered, and the first generation bore a second generation. Now, as he thought of all this, the priest had only one regret — that, ironically, the man responsible for all this had not himself changed.

Kriker.

His rage had been too deep somehow, his ways too instinctive and reckless, for even the accomplishment of the settlement to calm him.

And so only a month ago, they had struck a bargain, the priest and Kriker.

Kriker would be involved in one more robbery and then he would take his part of the proceeds and take the little girl and he would leave the settlement. Forever.

The people here were tired of being afraid of Kriker, and tired of being afraid that he would someday be responsible for the destruction of the settlement he had helped build.

Father Healy stood now as Kriker came up the small sand hill toward him. The day was raw. Kriker huddled into his sheepskin. He carried his carbine, as always.

Behind Kriker everything was gray. The grass and foliage were barren with winter. Smoke from chimneys curled from the roof of each cabin. The cows huddled together in the lean-to next to a long line of scrub oaks forming a windbreak.

Kriker said, "She ain't no better."

The priest could see tears in Kriker's eyes.

The priest sighed. "I'm sorry, Kriker."

"The granny woman even give her the rattlesnake heart."

The priest felt Kriker studying him. He knew that his disbelief in the granny woman's ways angered Kriker. "The girl needs a doctor."

Kriker hefted his carbine. "You ain't bringin' no doc out here, you understand?"

Carefully, for this was the first time the priest had said anything about the subject to anyone in the settlement: "There's a possibility we've got a problem on our hands."

"What kind of problem?"

"Other people are getting sick, too."

Kriker stared at him. "Like Maundy?"

"Just like Maundy."

"Maybe it's somethin' we eat. Meat maybe."

"Meat doesn't make people sick this way." The priest pulled himself to full height, about five-eight. Inside his dusty black cassock, he was a chunky man with white hair and blue eyes. Inexplicably, there was a knife scar just below his left ear. Nobody in the settlement could ever remember seeing a priest with a knife scar before. But the priest stayed and nobody asked questions. Given the background of the settlement itself, questions were kept to a minimum.

"We need a doctor," the priest said.

Kriker shook his head, waved his rifle at the encampment below. "By mornin' the granny woman will have Maundy fixed up and then we can travel. Two men are stoppin' by in the mornin' and then Maundy and I will be gone."

"Two men?" There was recrimination in the priest's voice. "I thought we had an agreement. We abide by the law here now, Kriker. That's why Sheriff Decker leaves us alone."

Kriker grinned. "Sheriff Decker. If he only knew."

"What sort of men are these?"

"Just the sort of men you'd expect me to be with, Father. Just that sort exactly."

"We can't afford trouble." The priest added, "You were part of it, weren't you?"

"Part of what?"

"You know what. That bank robbery in town."

"I needed a stake. For me and Maundy. We're headed west."

"You should find that girl a good family and leave her be."

Kriker's anger was quick and startling, and in it the priest could see the mountain-man ferocity that had made Kriker so frightening both in fact and in legend. He grabbed the priest by the shoulder and said, "I lost my real child and now all I've got is Maundy. A man ain't nothin' without his offspring. Nothin'. You understand me?"

He let the priest go.

The gray clouds, promising snow in the west, lay like fog on the tops of the pines in the mountains surrounding them. The wind was cold enough to make the priest's cheeks red.

"Them men are gonna be here, and then we're gonna split the money, and then they're gonna go one direction and me and Maundy's goin' another," Kriker said, "and then the settlement's all yours. You do anything you like with it."

This was Kriker's way of making peace after he had lost his temper. He never apologized. He merely made his voice gentler.

"You understand, Father?"

"I understand."

"You say some prayers for Maundy, too, you hear?"

"I will, Kriker. I will."

Kriker nodded and then returned to the settlement below, leaving the priest to think of the symptoms he'd encountered in the settlement the past few days, and of the word he hadn't heard since a single terrible spring a decade or so ago in St. Louis when 4,500 people had died of the same disease.

The word held unimaginable power for being such a simple few syllables.

Cholera.

CHAPTER SEVEN

It was land of ugly beauty, scoria buttes rising into rounded hills of red volcanic rock, hard ground littered with buffalo skulls bleached white by sun and now made even whiter by the snow that blew in the harsh northeasterly wind. Then there was the endless tireless prairie, untold miles of it, brown grass, the rusted ribs of deserted Conestoga wagons, and then an area of alkali desert and sagebrush spiny cactus, dead as a man's worst fear of what lay beyond death. Two emaciated magpies fed here on the fetid meat of a gangrened deer, and thin little creeks were already frozen in the gray twenty-degree afternoon weather that continued lashing the three riders with sticky blasts of wet snow.

They rarely spoke, James riding a grulla several lengths away, Thomas Bruckner and Guild back a ways, staying within a pace of each other. Obviously neither man wanted

51

the other behind him with a gun.

They stopped once to ride down into a gulley where they ate salt pork, beans, and bread, and drank water by kicking in a membrane of ice and scooping up creek water. Wind was trapped in here and it had a frightening majesty, chafing their faces, whistling off the volcanic rock that dinosaurs had once prowled. Still, they talked very little. Guild said, "How you planning to do this?"

"We're gonna go in at night and surprise him," Thomas Bruckner said. "Why?"

"Because I don't see any reason to shoot him."

"He killed two men, didn't he?"

Guild said, "Did he?"

"That supposed to mean something?"

Guild said nothing. He went back to his mount and adjusted the bedding he carried, and the oilskin coat in case things got very bad, and a small waterproof bag for personal things, among which was a picture of the little girl. He wasn't sure why he carried it. Once a priest had advised him to tear it up, but when Guild had tried he couldn't. It rode with him everywhere.

According to Guild's Ingram it was 3:18 when they started riding again.

■ ■ ■ ■

They found the Indian just before nightfall.

At first they weren't sure what it was. The prairie, flat, without detail, played more tricks than a desert. A man could look a quarter mile off and see something, and then before he reached it it would change apparent shape half a dozen times.

But they saw birds, crows and magpies mostly, and they didn't have to wonder much here in the now-drifting snow what it was. It might be a mule or a plump rabbit, but whatever it was it was most certainly flesh of some kind or the birds would not be here on the grasses. Light faded now, and everything on the ground was becoming white, and Guild's cheeks were red and numb and so he pulled a red bandanna robber-style across his face.

At least there was no smell, he thought, when they reached what proved to be the Indian.

He'd been an old man, gray-haired, toothless. The birds had eaten out his eyes and a part of his mouth and some of his belly.

Guild hefted his double 10-gauge with one gloved hand and shot at the birds to scare them off. There was no sense killing them. They were birds and they did what birds did and you could not judge them otherwise.

Thomas Bruckner raised his rifle and began firing, too.

It took Guild a moment, there in the dusk, to realize what Bruckner was shooting at.

Not the birds but the dead man.

He put four bullets in the dead Indian's forehead and then he laughed, "Sumbitch." He looked back to his burn-faced brother. "Indian sumbitch."

The Indian lay there in his garish rags, the kind white men gave red men on reservations. No telling what he'd been doing out here or what had killed him. Could have been anything from a heart attack to simply stumbling and cracking his skull.

"No call for that, Thomas," James Bruckner said. There was weariness and a certain resentment in his voice. "He's already dead."

Thomas Bruckner put one more bullet into the dead man. "Yeah," he said. "But he ain't dead enough." He looked at Guild.

They rode on to the settlement.

As they rode, James Bruckner kept thinking of how his brother had shot the dead man back there. He had started twitching, James had, the way he always twitched when his brother did something like this.

The way he had started twitching when, as small boys, Thomas had doused his little brother in kerosene and then thrown a match.

"Not near as bad as it could have been," the circuit doc had said, complimenting the missus on applying wet tea leaves to the boy. "Not as bad as it could have been. He didn't die."

But there were different ways to die, of course. You died when people laughed at you and pointed. You died when you knew you would never hold any but a house-bought woman.

There were a lot of different ways to die.

The sounds of his brother's rifle still echoed in his brain, as did his own screams from years ago when his brother had poured kerosene on him.

He tilted the brim of his hat lower.

The snow was getting bitter.

And he was still twitching, one involuntary spasm after another, a sight ugly in his own eyes as the leathery patch of burned skin covering half his cheek.

CHAPTER EIGHT

By Guild's Ingram it was 8:07 P.M. when they reached the top of the barren hill below which sprawled the valley where the settlement, in summer, yielded its bounty.

The noon was round and silver and alien. The tired horses crunched the icy earth and snorted wearily. Blowing snow was an off-white sheet covering everything, even the deep jet shadows cast by the jagged volcanic rock. Wind came like unearthly song down the mountains and across the silver shine of creek and the grassy cradle of cultivated land where only a month ago wheat yellow as gold had been scythed. But now there was just the wind and the rock and the three men sitting on their horses, staring at the settlement below.

Guild, leaning forward in his saddle, jerked the double 10-gauge from its scabbard. This was the surprise he'd been waiting to visit on the Bruckners ever since last night and the deaths of Rig and you Kenny Tolliver.

He put the double 10-gauge right to the burned part of James Bruckner's face and said, "I'll kill you right here if you don't both throw down your guns."

"What the hell you doin', Guild?" Thomas Bruckner said.

Into the wind, Guild said, "The way I read all this, you killed Rig and Tolliver so you could get your share of the bank money."

"What bank money?" Thomas Bruckner said.

"He knows, Thomas, he knows." Guild jabbed James Bruckner's face with the 10-gauge right where the burned area was. James Bruckner sounded ready to cry.

"You were all in it together. You and this Kriker and Rig and Tolliver," Guild said. "No easier trick than to have the law provide the lookout while the robbers empty out the bank."

"You'd really shoot him, Guild?" Thomas Bruckner said.

Guild pulled back the hammer. "You want to try me?"

"So what're you proposin'?"

"First your weapons get thrown and then I want you to get down."

"I don't think he's foolin', Thomas,"

James Bruckner said. His face was lost in the shadows beneath his hat rim, but you could hear his tears.

"You sumbitch," Thomas Bruckner said. "I knew you was trash. I knew it."

He threw down his rifle.

Guild said, "Now the guns and the knife."

"You sumbitch."

Then came the handguns and the knife.

Guild prodded James Bruckner with the double 10-gauge.

"Now you do the same."

"You're goin' to get it, James," Thomas Bruckner said, obviously needing to threaten somebody, and with Guild holding the gun there was no point in threatening him. "Just the way I used to give it to you in the barn when Pa was out in the fields. Just that way, James."

James threw down his weapons. They made a chinking sound against the volcanic rock.

Guild took the rope from his saddle and swung it over to James. "Now get down real easy and go over and tie your brother to that pine down the hill there."

James Bruckner said, "He'll kill me if I do, mister."

"I'll kill you if you don't."

"Oh, Jesus, mister, you're puttin' me in a

real pickle."

Guild prodded him with the gun again. "You walk down that hill and tie him up or I'll shoot you right here."

"He's just talkin', James. You don't listen to him."

"He shot a little girl, Thomas. Nobody who shoots a little girl is just talkin'."

Apparently Thomas now saw the inevitable. "This all over, James, you're gonna get it real good. Real, real good."

"Ain't my fault, Thomas. Ain't my fault."

Guild was tired of the talk. He walked the Appaloosa over to where Thomas Bruckner had dismounted. Guild slugged the man once, hard in the mouth.

"Jesus Christ, Jesus Christ!" Thomas Bruckner cried into the wind. He was holding a handful of thick blood. His own.

So his brother took him downhill and lashed him to the pine that grew on a slant on the snowy slope.

Guild dropped off the Appaloosa to check James Bruckner's handiwork. The man had done a good job.

Guild took a rope from Thomas Bruckner's grulla and then tied up James on the other side of the same tree.

"You sumbitch," Thomas Bruckner said.

"You sumbitch."

Guild rode into the settlement fifteen minutes later, coming down a grassy hill sleek with snow. Cinders from log fires cracked against the black night sky. The air was pleasantly smoky. Through pieces of burlap in windows you could see the reddish glow of fires and hear the soft crying of infants.

Guild, his double 10-gauge cradled in his right arm, dismounted.

In the center cabin, a door opened and a man in long black garb stood there. A priest.

He came forward into the gloom, his breath frosty, his left hand wrapped around a tin coffee cup.

"Good evening, sir," the priest said in a formal way.

"Good evening, Father."

"You wish a place to sleep tonight?"

"No," Guild said. "I'm looking for a certain man."

"Who would that be?"

"A man named Kriker."

"Kriker, I see."

"He's here, then?"

"No, I'm afraid he's gone."

"I didn't know priest told lies."

The priest paused, looked around. "You're

with the sheriff?"

"No."

The priest stared at him a long moment. A collie dog came up. He was covered with snow. He was panting. He looked like he was enjoying himself.

"You're a bounty man."

"Yes," Guild said.

"That is a shameful occupation."

"Where's Kriker?"

"He's not as bad as you may have heard."

"Some men were killed. He may have had something to do with it."

The priest frowned.

Guild lifted the double 10-gauge. "I want to speak with him, Father. Now."

Even from here, even from behind, Guild could hear the safety clicking off the rifle.

"You want to talk, bounty man? You got your chance."

Given the size and the wildness of the man who appeared in the center of the circle of cabins, Guild knew he was finally seeing Harry Kriker.

Bu apparently Kriker changed his mind, because just as Guild began to speak, Kriker brought his fist down hard on the back of Guild's head.

Guild was unconscious instantly, the collie dog mewling as Guild's face slammed to the ground and was partially buried in deep snow.

CHAPTER NINE

Thomas William Bruckner had been raised, along with six brothers and seven sisters, in a large soddie in the southernmost tip of the Territory, down where days were generally longer by forty-five minutes and temperatures generally warmer by ten degrees. He was the second brother in line and at once the wiliest. Even his older brother, Earle, had had the good sense to fear him. After age six, when Thomas had locked Earle in the barn with a boar widely known to have eaten at least ten piglets right down to the bone — and Thomas had sat on the roof watching Earle trying to get out of the barn as the boar continually charged at him — Earle had not only stayed out of Thomas's way but had deferred to him in any matter in which Thomas demanded deference.

About his sisters, he did not think much at all, good or bad, except to note that three of them had very large breasts and three of them had virtually no breasts at all, and the ones with breasts he occasionally tried to spy on when they took baths in the tin tub on nights before wagon rides to church. Of the six Bruckner brothers, only two had any interest in getting off the farm, the others being perfectly content (as were Pa and Ma) to stay here and farm land that yielded twenty-five cents a bushel for wheat (and half the time you had to take your share in trade). The highlight of the whole year, it seemed, was the agricultural society meeting, where you got to see such exciting things as a squash that weighed 148 pounds and "really took the rags off the bush" (as Pa always liked to say) and where prizes were awarded in categories as diverse as Three-year-old Steers and Oxens and Best Buggy and Best Pleasure Carriage and Best Double and Single Plow. For the women there was Best Shawl and Best Woolen Sheets and Best Roll Stair Carpeting and Best Woolen Knit Socks. None of this was the least tolerable for a boy who read, with difficulty (having gone only through the fourth grade), exciting newspaper accounts of what life on the frontier was like back in the raw and early fifties.

It was, surprisingly, his second youngest

brother, James, who joined him in long and fantastic talks out in the woods, where they put prairie grass in corncob pipes and smoked till their throats were raw and dreamed aloud of what life in frontier towns would be like. Surprisingly for two reasons. One, James was the slightest in size and ambition. Pa always said, "He's more comfortable doin' the woman's work," and so, in fact, he'd been. And surprisingly for a second reason, too — because even though Thomas had only been playing the day he'd thrown kerosene on James and then tossed a wooden match at the soaked ground around James just to scare him, he was amazed, given the ugliness of James's face, that James would have much to do with him.

But somehow James let Thomas become his boss, Thomas sensing that James did not know how to become as manly as his other brothers, and also sensing that James expected Thomas to teach him. So Thomas taught him to wrestle and shoot game and use a slingshot and make sly little jokes with the Indians who they'd see in the tiny four-buggy village where Pa sent them for certain store-bought provisions from time to time.

Then one April night, the air sweet with spring and prairie grasses already long and the moon bright as madness itself, Thomas, who was then sixteen, and James, who was then twelve, left the farm with such belongings as they could rightfully claim (though technically the hunting rifle belonged to the oldest brother, Earle) and set out to find that type of excitement peculiar to the Territory in those days.

What they found was exactly the opposite, of course. In town after town they worked in restaurants washing dishes or in livery stables with coloreds hauling manure or on farm crews for ten cents a day cutting grain with a cradle and binding it with a band of straw (a feat nobody today knew how to accomplish). Many times as they lay on hard cold ground, the stars chill and distant as their old dreams, James, now fourteen, would cry from loneliness and confusion or some pain a towny had put on him that day for the ugliness of his burned face; and even Thomas, remote and angry as he usually was, felt like crying, too, for what they'd found in the frontier towns were boys like themselves, long on dreams and short on money, comprising a kind of underclass of little more stature than Indians or runaway slaves, sleeping in lofts and alleys and tarp-covered wagons, and always waiting to be run in by bored or mendacious police officers.

Then Thomas William Bruckner shot and killed his first man and everything changed abruptly and much for the better.

It happened up near the Montana border, and actually it happened by mistake. The Bruckner brothers were in a tavern where men fought as much for pleasure as passion and where every sort of illegal dead — from theft to murder — could be planned and a man found to carry out the plan. Thomas William Bruckner was now twenty. He had lost, in the past year, three teeth in four fist-fights, a cache of fifty-seven dollars he'd managed to save from farm work, and his virginity. This had happened in a fancy house, and of course he'd gotten the clap and it had all ended in about fifteen excited seconds anyway. She'd looked relieved. An easy fifty cents for fifteen seconds.

Anyway. The tavern.

A man, quite large and quite drunk, had accosted another man, making delirious accusations about the other's advances toward his wife.

The larger man, even though he did not need any help in defeating the smaller one, began to take out a pistol, his certain intent to kill the smaller man.

It was at this moment that Thomas William Bruckner, standing down the bar, tried to get out of the way of the gunfire, and in so doing instinctively drew his own Peace-maker. And then he tripped. The floor was crude pine and the ten-penny nails had not been nailed flat and the toe of his boot had caught the nub of a nail and —

— and his Peacemaker fired and he shot exactly in the heart the large man who had been about to shoot exactly in the heart the smaller man and —

— and it turned out that the smaller man was a good friend of the man who virtually ran the town — or anyway ran those things in the town that mattered, which was to say the women and the liquor and the labor force.

And so it was that the Bruckner brothers learned what the frontier was all about. Not heroic or legendary gun battles. Not the beauty of the sprawling Territory. Not the sense of holding your own destiny in your own hands. Control: that's what the frontier was really all about.

So the Bruckners went to work for the man who controlled the town, and then they moved on to another, larger town where another, more powerful man decided what went on and what didn't go on, and they worked for him, doing jobs large and small, including occasionally killings.

Thomas became particularly good at running a shakedown business — offering protection from the law to people who ran whorehouses and saloons, and that was easy enough to do because the first person you always paid off in any town was the lawman.

This was all ten years earlier. There had been a marriage that ended — or so Thomas said — when the woman had fallen down the stairs the night before. (James knew better than to talk about what he'd seen.) There had been some arson in Chicago in which forty Chinese had died and a man named Fitzsimmons got the block he'd been after at the price he'd been waiting to pay. The brothers had hated Chicago, having, like most Territory people, an equal aversion to slavery and to black people. Finally there had been innumerable jobs for innumerable lawmen in innumerable small towns where whores were sold on the hoof and almost any kind of violence could be disguised as accidental.

James himself had killed only once. Thomas had gutshot a saloon owner who'd refused to pay protection. As the man was gagging and puking his last, Thomas, quite calmly, had handed James the rifle and said, "You need the experience, brother. Now you go on and do it, hear me?" James shook his head and backed away and refused to do it. And he would have kept on refusing, only the man was in such misery — this is what he told Thomas later — that he reckoned he was doing him a favor, so he took the rifle and cocked it and shot the man twice in the face, exploding his brain, and then he was just one more dead animal and there was no more pain for him.

These were the Bruckner brothers, the two lashed now to the pine tree on the downslope in the hammered-silver moonlight and the white whipping snow.

"I'm gonna put that gun as far up his ass as it'll go," Thomas Bruckner said, making obvious reference to Guild. "Then I'm just gonna keep loadin' and reloadin' till my arms get tired."

The wind took his voice and made it vanish down the piny slope of volcanic rock.

CHAPTER TEN

He was in a cabin in a straight-backed chair, and Kriker stood over him with a gun. The cabin smelled of cooked meat and illness. In a corner on the cot, in shadows cast by a kerosene lamp, lay a little girl beneath several layers of buffalo hides. You could see by the way she sweated and by the flat white of her skin and by the fever blisters on her tiny gentle mouth that she was very very ill.

Kriker slapped Guild once clean and hard across the side of the face. Guild started to get up out of the chair — anger over being slapped hurting his pride — but then through the door the priest came and he looked at both of them and said, "Kriker. You said there would be no violence."

Kriker set his Sharps down and said, "I want to know why he's here."

"You know why. He's a bounty man." The priest nodded to Guild, and said to Kriker, "You should take that as a sign. You should take your money and leave. With winter coming they won't find you in Canada."

"I won't leave without her."

"She can't travel," the priest said.

Guild sensed how softly the priest spoke when the subject of the girl came up. Obviously he was afraid of infuriating Kriker.

"Where's the granny woman?" Kriker demanded.

"The granny woman can't help."

"She knows the secrets."

"There are no secrets, Kriker. Except for a medical doctor."

"No!" Kriker said, leaning toward the priest.

As Guild watched them talk, he noticed that the priest was missing the final two fingers on his right hand. When he gestured with the hand, the movement gave the man an odd vulnerability. But beyond that, something else troubled Guild. He knew there was some significance to the missing fingers but he did not know what. Something he was failing to remember . . .

Guild said, "I've got the Bruckner brothers tied to a tree."

Kriker turned back to him. "The Bruckner brothers?"

Guild nodded. "I'd like to get up, Kriker. I've got a bad headache from where you hit me. I'd like to get up and have some coffee and walk around."

"I want you to tell me about the Bruckner brothers. What the hell are you doing with them?"

Guild looked to the priest, who said, "Let him have some coffee and walk around. You have the gun, Kriker. He's unarmed."

Kriker glared at Guild, but then he nodded approval.

The priest got Guild some coffee and poured it into a chipped china cup that he handled with some reverence — people this poor in the Territory valued beyond reason chipped castoffs from the rich that they bought in second-hand stores where they stood in line with handcuffs of pennies to buy bitter bits of real civilization. While the priest was busy with Guild, Kriker went over and knelt by the girl.

She moaned and Guild saw Kriker jerk back as if he'd been shot. In that simple movement Guild sensed how much the mountain man loved the little girl.

Kriker took a pitcher of water from the nightstand and filled a glass and then raised the girl's head and gave her a drink.

Guild saw tears shine in Kriker's eyes.

Guild looked back at the priest. "She been throwing up?"

"Yes."

"Drinking a lot of water?"

The priest nodded.

"Bad intestinal cramps?"

"Yes, Mr. Guild. Why?"

Guild's face grew tight in the soft lamplight. He did not want to say the word. He did not want to see the pain on Kriker's face.

In a whisper, Guild said, "You know what's going on here, Father."

"Yes."

"But he doesn't, apparently."

"No."

Kriker was talking to the girl.

Guild said, "You need to get a doctor out here right away."

"I know."

Kriker got up, came over. "She seems to be doing better."

He wanted them to agree.

The priest said, "Maybe that's so, Kriker."

"We'll bundle her up. I can take her with me tonight."

Guild said, "She can't travel, Kriker."

"What the hell you talking about?

"She's got cholera."

There was no other way around it now. He had to look away from Kriker.

Kriker said to the priest, "What the hell's

he talking about?"

"He's right, Kriker. She's got cholera and so do several other people in the settlement. We're having a meeting in half an hour." The priest paused. "That's why we need you to clear out. Because we've got to bring in a doctor, and when he sees the cholera, he'll bring in the law. They'll want to make sure this doesn't spread any farther than it has to."

"I won't leave without her."

The priest touched Kriker's arm. The huge man in the dirty buckskins and the wild hair looked lost suddenly — as if his eyes could not focus, his tongue and lips unable to form words.

The priest said, "They're going to vote."

"Who is?"

"The people of the settlement."

"On what?"

"On you."

"Me?"

"Whether to force you out."

"I founded this place. I felled the trees and cleared the fields. There wouldn't be any settlement if it wasn't for me."

"But now you can destroy it, Kriker, and you can't see that. The law is looking for you because they think you killed two men in town and that means they'll destroy this settlement to get you."

Kriker swung around to Guild. "Is this why you come out here, bounty man?"

Guild said, "Yes."

"They're offering a reward because I'm supposed to have killed two men."

"Yes."

"What men?"

"Rig and Tolliver."

"Rig and Tolliver? I didn't kill them."

"I know you didn't. But the Bruckner brothers have convinced the sheriff you did, and they came out here to take you in."

"They'd shoot me."

"Sure they would, Kriker. First chance."

"I didn't kill them men."

"I know."

Kriker said, "Shit," and slammed his right fist into the palm of his left hand. He glanced at the girl. "I've got to get her out of here."

"Why don't you go back with me?" Guild said.

"What?"

"Talk to Decker. I'll make sure the Bruckners don't get to you, and you can tell your side of things."

"I helped stick up the bank. Me and Rig planned it. Tolliver and the deputies was part of it."

76

"Tell that to Decker."

"They'll still arrest me for robbery."

Guild said, "It's easier than running, Kriker. You're not young anymore and running isn't easy. It isn't easy at all."

Kriker, still seeming dazed by the events of the past half hour, said, "They need to get to me."

"Who?"

"The Bruckners."

"Why?"

"Because I got the bank money hid."

"Why don't you turn it over to me?"

For the first time, Kriker laughed. "You're some hopped-up sonabitch, aren't you? You goddamn bounty men. A little girl is layin' here sick and two deputies are coming to kill me and all you can think about is the reward."

"Winter's coming," Guild said. "I'm no younger than you and I need money." He shrugged. "It's my job." He nodded to the priest. "Besides, the priest is right. If you don't want to deal with Decker, then you should leave clean. Pack up and head out fast. By the time the Bruckners and Decker catch up with you, you'll be long gone."

"How come you don't want to take me in?

"I want the robbery money. I return that,

I've got my reward. Plus I think I can convince Decker that you didn't have anything to do with killing Rig or the Tolliver kid. I owe the kid and his mother that much."

Kriker glanced at the sleeping girl. She was moaning again, her face white except for the cheeks where the fever was deep red fire.

Kriker said, seeming to forget everything they'd been talking about, "She needs some more water."

He went over to her and poured another glass and then knelt down.

He touched her head, kissing her, and this time there could be no mistaking the sounds he made.

Kriker was sobbing.

He was old enough to remember when a white Canadian named Theophile Brughier had married the daughter of the Dakota Sioux Chief War Eagle and thereby brought a measure of peace, however temporary, to the area.

He was old enough to remember when Indian women did the gardening with antler rakes and hoes made from bison shoulders.

He was old enough to remember when Indians were not farmers at all but were hunters. It was the white man and his reservations who had turned hunter into farmer, and failed farmer at that, for now Indians not only his age but Indians small as infants waited in line at army posts for scraps of food and the quick pitying smile of the blue-coated supply sergeant.

He was old enough to remember when he could have erections he did not even want and old enough to remember what this part of the Territory had been like before the buffalo were killed and before the blue sky was crosshatched with telephone and electrical poles and before the river bore the taint of ore from the factory waters upstream.

His name was Pa-wa-shi-ka and he was coming to see his friend, the priest at the settlement. The seventy-nine-year-old Indian had begun coughing up blood again, and last time the priest had told him to come at once if this happened again.

So even tonight in this cold without mercy, he had left his soddie downstream and come up onto the area of rock, his dun slipping on the soft snow, up over the hill, and down to the settlement below.

At first he imagined the sickness that came with the coughing blood was playing tricks on his ears. That and the whipping wind.

Hunched down inside the robes, he imag-

79

ined he could hear sounds. Desperate sounds. Human sounds.

He stuck his face outside the robe draped over his head.

In the cutting snow, it was almost impossible to see. Even given the curious silver illumination of the full moon.

He did not see the men at first. He did not even see the tree.

He merely continued on up the rocky hill, his dun now no faster than an aged burro.

Then for a moment — as if a fabric had been torn and his gaze allowed to see inside — he saw the two men lashed to the scrubby pine tree on the deep slope of the hill.

At first he did not slow the course of his dun at all. The two men were white, and he had learned long ago never to become involved in a white man's affair unless you had absolutely no choice. White men were crazed, and even those who seemed friendly were capable of turning on you suddenly, the way animals suddenly and for no reason turn on humans.

He went on.

But they continued yelling, their voices slapping at him on the downdraft of the snow wind, and so finally he reined the dun to a stop and turned around and peeked out of his robe again at the two men.

"We won't make it through the night, Grandpa!" one of them shouted. "Please help us out."

Pa-wa-shi-ka turned his horse to the right, toward the tree. He had a coughing fit then and simply let the horse walk over by the tree.

"Who tied you up?" the Indian asked from his horse.

The two men writhed against their lashes. The one without the burned face said, "Robbers. We're deputies and they captured us. You help us out, Grandpa, and we'll see that you get part of the reward."

The old man shook his head. "It is not good to help white people. They turn on you."

"Please," said the one with the burned face. "We won't last the night. It'll get in our lungs and we'll die of pneumonia."

"Look at my goddamn jacket, old man," the other white man said, shouting above the wind. It was as if they were in a tunnel and the tunnel was roaring with wind.

And then the Indian saw it. The shine of silver — the white man's badge of authority.

"You are law?"

"Law. Yes. Jesus." The man without the burns sounded frantic.

81

"I will be in trouble if I don't help you, then," the old man decided.

"Very bad trouble," the man without the burns said.

Pa-was-shi-ka began choking with a cough spasm again.

Finally he got down from his dun and went over to the two lashed men and cut them free.

The man without the burn did not wait long. He grabbed the Indian's knife away from him and then said, "I want your rifle there, Grandpa."

"My rifle?"

"And your horse."

"Horse? But why?"

But the white man said nothing. He simply walked over to the horse, helped the other white man up, and left Pa-wa-shi-ka standing there to think of the days when he had been a hunter and when nobody would ever have been able to take his knife that way, let alone steal his rifle and horse.

But then he fell to coughing and the blood was thick and hot now, spilling down the front of his cotton shirt.

He went over and picked up the hide robe they had flung from the dun as they'd set off up the hill.

The Indian wrapped himself in the robe

and started off walking.

The way he was coughing, he wondered it he would have strength enough to reach the settlement.

CHAPTER ELEVEN

The bird was a barn swallow trapped by the granny woman fifteen minutes ago and brought here to the cabin where the sick girl lay.

The priest had gone several cabins away, where the meeting between the settlement people was taking place.

Kriker with his rifle and Guild with his sense of helplessness stayed here. Sometimes he watched the little girl and then recalled the little girl he'd shot. Life was fragile enough, but for children it was doubly so. He thought of small hands reaching out with no grasp strong enough to save them.

Kriker, now sitting by the girl in a chair angled so that he could watch Guild with no problem, said to the granny woman, "You better hurry up. She's hotter than she was an hour ago."

"I got no guarantees, Kriker."

"You said you could handle it all right."

"I said I could handle it all right if the demons wasn't in her." She shrugged aged shoulders. "If the demons is in her, ain't much I can do."

"A doc could help," Guild said. "She needs a doc."

"You shut up, bounty man. I'm sick of you already." Kriker glared up at the granny woman. The kerosene lamp still cast strong shadows and the wind slammed like a fist against the burlap of cabin windows.

The girl started up in bed abruptly and began vomiting. Guild went over to her and without a word held her frail little shoulders as the puking jerked her about. Kriker held a pan under her mouth.

When she was done and Kriker had laid her back down again, he looked at Guild and said, as if surprised by Guild's tenderness, "Thanks."

"She's a nice little girl."

"She's a beautiful, lonely little girl. She never complains." The he dropped his gaze to her again and shook his head and whispered "Son of a bitch" at whatever gods he held responsible for this.

The brown barn swallow was little more than a chick, and so the area of its breast was small and the location of its heart difficult to find. "I'm gonna need one of you to hold this bird for me," the granny woman said.

Kriker said, "I'll do it."

He got up and went over to the table where the granny woman worked. He clamped big hands on the tiny bird that gazed up at him with terrified alien eyes.

The granny woman stabbed the bird in the breast area. Some kind of mucus ran out of the bird's mouth. The eyes grew very large and then a thin membranous haze covered its gaze and then it was dead.

The granny woman worked efficiently now. She cut out the innards and searched with hard white hands through the soft red innard until she came to the heart, which was smaller than a pea. She had been boiling milk in a pan on a small fire in the corner. She took the hot milk and poured some in a tin coffee cup and then dropped the tiny heart into the burned crust of milk floating on top.

Guild shook his head. It was too late on the frontier for anybody reasonable to still practice granny medicine, and yet tens of thousands of people still did. Day in and day out their patients died after drinking tea made of water and the cleaved-off tail of a black cat or eating a handful of fish worms or tying the nail of a coffin to a foot to take care of rheumatism.

The little girl was dying and they were feeding her the heart of a barn swallow. He hated them for their mountain-born stupidity and yet he was moved by their grief and their earnestness.

"You hold her head and I'll pour it down her," the granny woman said.

"This better work," Kriker said.

"It will, Kriker," the granny woman said.

But she glanced anxiously at Guild, and he saw that she looked afraid because she knew what Kriker would do to her if the girl died.

The granny woman stuck a stick in the tin cup. "We want to get the blood good and stirred," she said.

"Good and stirred," said Kriker. He sounded dazed again.

They went over and gave the girl the heart of the barn swallow.

Guild looked back at the bird's carcass on the table. The blood didn't bother him so much as the eyes. They were open and staring, and he went over and closed them.

The little girl puked up the milk less that three minutes after they give it to her.

He was not really a priest, of course, and

those in the settlement knew it. He had come here eight years ago, the law back in Chicago interested in his part in the murder of a cardsharp (John Healy was himself a cardsharp), but he found both himself and the settlement in need of a priest and so he became one.

At first they did not honor him. They would scoff and curse and deride him. But a woman, whose baby strangled at bloody birth, was comforted by the fake priest, as was her husband, and so Healy made two converts among the forty or so settlement people. Then a woman asked Healy to baptize her infant and then a man asked him to give his consumptive wife last rites. And then, Healy having long worn the black cassock and white collar now, children began calling him "Father." There came a flood and Healy offered succor as well as prayers spoken in a tongue touched with brogue, manly and fine, here in the forest where they'd fled. And at planting season he stood as Jesus had stood, arms wide and praying to the blue sky for bountiful harvest and the balm of friendship. By then even the adults had come to call him Father Healy, and now there was no question that he was a priest. The settlement, wanting its own form of civilization, wanting its children to learn the secrets of print on paper and the ways of men who did not beat their wives and work their children as slaves — the settlement had forgotten utterly about a man named Healy who'd been a Chicago cardsharp. They knew only a Healy who was a priest, and a good one.

Father Healy himself had only one problem with his role. He knew the society necessity of the settlement having a priest, yet he did not believe in God. He tried. He held the most delicate flowers and splashed in his hands the purest of water and watched unblinking the steep and unfaltering arc of the hawk against the blue summer sky. He saw all the evidence of a God, and yet in his heart he could not believe in one.

He blamed this on his boyhood near the Union Stockyards in Chicago, where his father came home day after numbed day bloody as a stillborn babe, the entrails of dead animals clinging to him like the white larvae of maggots to spoiled meat. What a place the Union Stockyards had been. Two million dollars to construct. Three hundred fifty-five acres alone of cattle pens. And the animals themselves. Twenty-five thousand cattle. Eighty thousand hogs. Twenty-five thousand sheep. All this carrying the stench and sound of hell itself, for it was estimated that ten thousand animals a day died there, that on some killing floors the blood was so deep it splashed the knees in waves.

This was how the young Healy came to think of life and death. The men who owned the yards got you and they killed at their whim. And then, as with the sad-eyed cows and the plump pink pigs and the sweet frightened lambs — then there was just the darkness. Just the darkness.

He had been forced to be a priest because he saw early on that he had none of the skills the other settlement men could claim. He was too clumsy for farm work and too unskilled for building. But he spoke in his fine voice and he knew how to read, and his gambling days had left him with gift for reassuring others (nobody needing more reassurance than a man you were cheating), and so it was that Healy followed in the footsteps of Jesus and tried to believe in Jesus but did not — even on the most overpowering of star-flung spring nights — much as he so desperately prayed to.

But it was important for him to be a priest because there was no other thing he could be for this settlement, and it was important for the settlement to have him be its priest because even the strongest of men were frightened of the things that lay just beyond daylight. So his words soothed them the way a baby is soothed in the lap and arm, even though the words are often meaningless to the parent uttering them, just soft imbecile songs of reassurance on the long night's air.

During all this time, Kriker had been the unquestioned master of the settlement and great deference had been paid to him.

But now, years of his robberies, years of the settlement's dreading an invasion by law, had come to an end because now the settlement was faced with something that not even Kriker's rage could manage — the prospect of cholera.

Crowded into the largest cabin now — the cabin usually used for meetings — were twenty men and women dressed in shabby winter clothes, shirt piled on shirt, town gloves pulled over raw knuckles. Yet in all there was a sense of purpose and pride that their stay at the settlement here had given them. They had been thieves and worse, and now they knew the satisfaction of real work. They had been plunderers, and now they knew the joy of having families and protecting that most precious gift of all, children.

And now they stood facing Kriker. Father Healy was between him and the others, while Kriker leaned against one corner of the cabin, smoking a cob pipe, his face drained of its unusual animation because only five minutes before he had seen that the girl's condition continued to deteriorate.

A man named Silas, a man big as Kriker himself in bib overalls and a red wool sweater, said, "We owe you our lives, Kriker. We're not meanin' to be ungrateful."

Kriker said, "I can't leave now. The girl's too sick to travel."

A woman said, without anger, "Kriker, we need a doc. The granny woman can't help us. And when the doc comes the law'll come, too, because they think you murdered those people in town. You know there been some people in town just waitin' to burn this place down. We don't want to give them no excuses, Kriker."

Kriker came away from the wall and glared at them — the young, the old, the lame among them, and the strong. They'd been his people, his flock, as it were, all these years, and now they regarded him as stranger.

"It's our settlement, Kriker," said another man. He was bald and wore a rough denim jacket and rough denim jeans. "You kept to the old ways — the ways we fled. But we learned the land, Kriker, and now those are our ways. We don't rob no more, and we don't have no law on us."

Kriker's grief turned to anger as he leaned on his Sharps. "You think I couldn't kill you, Jonathan?"

"You could kill me, Kriker." The man waved his hand to the others. They had guns of various kinds, too. "But you couldn't kill them."

Father Healy said, "We need to remember two things here. Without Kriker there would be no settlement. Each of us owes him more than we can say. Isn't that right?"

He addressed the group of them. Heads hung now, both with shame and with an obvious sense that perhaps the priest was going to try and peruade them not only to let Kriker stay, but to put off sending somebody for a doc in town.

"Isn't that right?" Father Healy repeated.

He was chastising them, the way a parent scolds children.

"Right," somebody at the back of the group said.

Then most of the people took it up, there in the cabin with the potbellied stove and the walls lined with jars of strawberry preserves and corn and string beans. There were quilts here, too, warm and beautiful ones, and a fiddle in the corner that sang sweetly on nights of festivity — and what Healy did with his words and hard glances was remind the people of who in the first place was responsible for all this.

Kriker.

Then the priest surprised everybody by turning to Kriker and saying, "But as grateful as we are Kriker, I have to put the good to everybody ahead of your own good."

Kriker seemed to sense what was coming.

The priest said, "You must leave tonight."

"Without the girl?"

"She can't travel, Kriker."

"You're supposed to be my friends."

"There are other children here, Kriker, and the threat of cholera. That comes before anything."

Kriker started to heft his gun.

Guild, who had been rolling a cigarette in the corner and just watching the proceedings, said, "The way cholera moves, you should send somebody right now."

"Tonight?" a man asked.

Guild nodded. "With the best horse you've got." Guild stood up and started edging toward Kriker because he could see what was about to happen. Kriker was getting ready to raise his Sharps.

Guild moved then, grabbing a chair and smashing it across the back of Kriker's head just as the man raised the Sharps.

Several people screamed, and for the next

few moments there was great confusion as Guild threw himself down on the still-conscious Kriker. Guild needed to get a punch off clean and hard enough to knock the man out completely.

The man named Jonathan saved him the trouble by coming over and kicking Kriker in the side of the head.

Kriker's head slammed against the floor. He was unconscious. Guild got his handcuffs from his gun belt and cuffed Kriker and then dragged him over to the wall.

When he got up he saw the man named Jonathan standing there staring down at Kriker. "I don't want to do that." He sounded on the verge of tears. "We owe him everything."

"You didn't have any choice," Guild said. To the priest he said, "Now let's get a rider. We need a doc and we need Sheriff Decker and a few deputies out here. One of you a good rider?"

He looked at the group and they pushed forth a young woman in braids and freckles. She was maybe sixteen. "She's the best," the priest said. He smiled affectionately. "She likes horses better than people."

"Yeah, all except for Jim Courtner over to the other village," a voice from the rear said. "She likes him best."

The young woman blushed.

"You think you can reach town in this storm?" Guild asked.

She nodded.

"All right," Guild said, "here's what you need to tell Decker, and here's what you need to tell the doc."

CHAPTER TWELVE

Thomas Bruckner crouched next to a pine just on the edge of the settlement.

His brother James, walking on his haunches, came up from behind. James said, "Maybe he won't give a damn about her anymore."

"You heard the way he'd talked about her to Rig and Tolliver."

The moonlight sparkled through the blowing snow. Thomas Bruckner's eyebrows were white with the freezing stuff.

James said, "It wouldn't be right."

Which was what Thomas had been waiting to hear — the thing that was really bothering his brother. Ever since Thomas had suggested taking the girl and using her as a way of getting the bank money from Kriker, James had been acting the way he usually did when he didn't want to do something but was afraid to say so.

A spindle-legged doe appeared in the

moonlit clearing. Then, sensing the two men, it took off faster than seemed possible west of the cabins.

Thomas said, "You want to make me mad?"

"You know better'n that, Thomas."

"Then you do what I say."

"She's a little girl."

Thomas wiped snow from his face, then sighed. "You remember that time in Kansas City?"

"What time?"

"The time with the red-haired woman who said you were ugly."

James waited a very long time before speaking as he crouched there next to her brother. "Yes," he said. "Yes, I remember."

"You remember what I did for you?"

Nothing.

"You remember, James?"

"Yes, I remember."

"Well, you think it's right that I'd do something like that for you, and here I ask you a simple little favor and you won't do nothin' for me at all?"

Nothing.

"You think that's right, James?"

"No, I guess not."

"I wish you'd say that louder so's I'd know you mean it."

"No, I guess it isn't right."

"I cut up her face real good for you, didn't I?"

"I didn't want you to do that, Thomas."

"But I did it."

"I didn't even want you to do it."

"But I love you, James. You're my brother and I love you and that's why I was obliged to do it."

"If you loved me, maybe you wouldn't have thrown that kerosene on me in the first place."

"I thought we had that agreement."

Nothing.

"I thought we had that agreement."

"I'm sorry."

"I thought we had that agreement that said I feel so bad about throwin' that kerosene on you that I never want to hear about it again."

"I'm sorry."

"But about once every couple weeks you go and break that agreement. You ever noticed how you do that, James?"

"I'm sorry, Thomas."

"Now I cut up that whore for you and it seems to me that the least thing you could do for me is go in there and get that little girl and bring her back out here while I stand guard. Doesn't that seem like the least little thing you could do for me?"

"I guess so."

"You don't sound sure."

"Sometimes I'm not sure, Thomas. Sometimes I'm not sure about anything."

The wind came again, and the freezing snow, silver dust devils of it now. Thomas said, "There's a line shack about a mile from here. We'll take her there and we'll all be nice and warm. Then we'll tell Kriker we've got her and then we'll get the money and then you and me can head for California."

"You shouldn't have cut her."

"Hell," Thomas Bruckner said. "Hell if I shouldn't have." Then, in to the smell of fire and human warmth downwind on the shadowy night, he said, "You go get her, James. You go get her right now."

Once he reached the camp, James Bruckner felt a familiar fear — that of desertion. As a boy he'd been lost in a rainstorm and he'd felt that he would never find his way home again. He felt surrounded by hostile entities he could not see. But then his brother Thomas had come looking for him and had guided him home.

Now James felt surrounded by hostile entities again. Only these he could see — or at least glimpse: the people of the settlement. People whose eyes would settle on the burned part of his face and narrow in disgust. People who would snicker and point behind his back. People who could never see what he was — but only what he appeared to be. Ever since being doused with the kerosene, he had imagined that people wanted to get their hands on him, to tear him apart the way a lynch mob had torn apart a black man in Keokuk one day when he and Thomas had been riding through, literally rending the man with their fingers and fists.

If the people of this settlement caught him stealing the girl, then the same fate would be his.

For the next ten minutes, he went cabin to cabin. In three cabins mothers sat with broods of children, humming, knitting, rocking infants. In one cabin an older man sat reading a yellow paperbound book by kerosene lamp.

In the fourth and largest of all the cabins, he heard the meeting taking place and heard what the settlement people were saying about Kriker, and what Kriker said about the little girl.

From this, James Bruckner learned what he should be looking for — a young girl who was sick from something, though he could not quite decide what from the conversation.

So he set about checking out other cabins, and finally he came to the one where an old woman sat in a rocking chair next to a cot where a fevered-looking young girl lay asleep.

The old woman held in her right hand, by its tiny feet, a dead bird which she was switching back and forth over the face of the sleeping girl.

A granny woman, James Bruckner realized.

He leaned back from the burlap window and pressed himself against the rough bark of the cabin wall as he heard feet crunching through the ice and snow.

His heart hammered as he thought of the black man in Keokuk and what the mob had done to him, what it wanted to do to anybody who was different from itself.

The crunching feet drew closer.

Cherry pipe smoke trailed on the night air.

The moon was so round and clear, even through the haze of snow, it looked unreal.

He pressed himself against the wall so hard the back of his head hurt from the pressure.

Please just go on by. Please just go on by.

Which is what they did, finally, two men, one of whom said, "I never seen Kriker like that. The way he looked back there."

"He looked old."

"It's the girl. It's like she's his own."

"She's never spoken since the day he took her. Never a word."

"He shouldn't have taken her. He should have left her."

"Never a word."

Then they were gone and James Allan Bruckner knew that he needed to move quickly now.

He yanked his Navy Colt from his holster — the leather sodden with snow — and walked carefully around to the front door of the cabin.

He moved almost without sound, having become, during his years since leaving home, very good at jobs that required stealth. Or at least that's what Thomas always told him when he insisted it was James Allan who should go into this place or that while Thomas stood some distance away "watching out."

He eased in the door, and before the granny woman quite had time to look up, he had the Colt aimed straight at her face and the hammer cocked.

"I don't want to hurt you, granny woman."

She had frozen now, holding the dead bird still above the sleeping girl's face.

"I just want the girl."

"Oh, no," the granny woman said. "This is Kriker's girl."

"I need to take her, granny woman. I need to take her and I want to do it without hurtin' you. Do you understand me?"

"She's Kriker's girl," the granny woman said again.

But for the moment, James Bruckner wasn't listening. He had been so long out in the bitter cold — first lashed to the tree and then hiding out on the edge of the settlement — that now all he could do was stare at the warm and comfortable cabin. There was food in the pantry — bread and rice and beans — and there was a potbelly stove and a tin tub for soaking in steamy hot water and a beautiful painting of the Lord and —

And the granny woman was staring at his face.

He sense it and his head snapped around and then his eyes confirmed it.

Obviously fascinated and repelled at the same time, the granny woman rested her eyes on his patch of burned skin.

Most people couldn't.

"What happened to your face?"

"Why would you care?" He sounded mean now.

" 'Cause I might know a treatment for it."

"There ain't no treatment for it."

"You sure?"

"I'm sure. Knew this granny woman in Wisconsin. She said there was a treatment for it and she spent several days tryin' but it came to nothin'." Then softly, "Nothin'."

"She try a robin's egg?"

"Yep."

"She try tyin' a mackerel to your head?"

"Yep."

"She try a —"

"She tried everything. Everything."

The granny woman, small but not at all frail, sat back in her rocking chair thoughtfully. "What you goin' to do with her?"

"Can't see how that's your business."

"You're shiverin'."

"I'm cold."

"You're shiverin' 'cause you're scared, too. You don't really want to take this little girl."

"Got to."

"Why?"

"Like I said, can't see how that's any of your business."

"She's got the cholera."

Without moving his Colt from the granny

woman's face, he eased his gaze to the girl. She almost looked dead, so still and pale. Only the sweat on her face spoke of fevered life.

"I got to take her, granny woman."

"She'll die if you move her."

"I got to take that chance."

"You know what Kriker'll do to you?"

"Help me git her bundled up, granny woman."

"It's gonna be terrible, what Kriker's gonna do."

"Help me git her bundled up," he said.

She helped him. She tugged a heavy woolen coat on the girl and then boots and then mittens and then a heavy woolen scarf around her head.

The first time James Bruckner touched her, he felt how hot the girl was. He couldn't see how anybody could be that hot and still be alive. He thought of cholera and the stories he'd heard about it and of a marshal he'd known who'd been fine at nine one morning and then dropped straight down dead at four that afternoon.

Cholera.

He hefted the girl under his arm like a bundle and said, "I'm gonna have to put you out, granny woman."

"Hit me?"

"Yep."

"You don't sound like you want to do that."

"Ain't a matter of want. Matter of need."

Which is when he struck her. He had learned over the years how to hit somebody just to put them out briefly and how to hit somebody to hurt them. She would not be out more than ten or fifteen minutes the way he'd just done her, and then all she'd have at worst would be a headache. He had only made a mistake once, in a Northeastern Territory town where Thomas had briefly been sheriff, when he'd hit a Mexican prisoner. The man had had epilepsy and had gone into convulsions right there at James Allan's feet. And he had died at James Allan's feet, too, and not for months could James Allan forget it, the way the man had spewed silver froth from his mouth, the crazed animal eyes, and the entire twitching body.

James Allan Bruckner hefted the girl under his arm and ran out into the night.

CHAPTER THIRTEEN

Guild got Kriker set up in a chair, still handcuffed, of course, and then got himself set up in a chair and then had a cigar while he waited for the big man to come to.

By now the others had left the central cabin. Guild sat there listening to the fire pop inside the potbellied stove and to the way the snow sounded like salt granules sprayed against the west side of the cabin.

When Kriker made a noise, Guild said, "I need you to tell me where the money is."

Kriker made no intelligible response. He moved his head from side to side as if he were in a great deal of pain, and then he said, "The girl."

"The granny woman's with her."

He was coming awake now, Kriker was. "She all right?"

"She needs a doc, Kriker. The priest is right."

"He ain't a priest."

"What?"

"He ain't a priest."

"He wears a cassock and a collar."

"He still ain't no priest."

"What is he, then?"

"Cardplayer from Chicago."

"I'll be damned," Guild said, and knew instantly who the man was. The missing fingers became a wanted poster and the wanted poster became a man. A cardsharp wanted for second-degree murder in the death of another cardsharp. Guild had one of those memories. He didn't recall everything about the poster — couldn't, for example, recall the amount of the reward — but he remembered the words "cardsharp" and "missing fingers."

But now that wasn't so important as the robbery money. To get that reward, all Guild needed to do was ride back to Sheriff Decker. To claim the priest he'd have to go all the way back to Chicago.

He said, "You're being selfish, Kriker."

"What's that supposed to mean?"

"The girl. She needs a doc and you need to let her go."

"She's my daughter."

"She's your daughter the way Healy is a priest."

"Her folks got killed and I took care of her."

"She needs a doc."

"A doc killed my wife and son."

Guild sighed. "They told me what happened, and it doesn't sound like it was the doc. It sounds like it was the disease."

"What disease?"

"Same one as this one. Cholera."

"She's got a touch of the bug is all."

"You know better."

"Hell."

"Hell, too," Guild said, "and you know it." He paused. "Where's the money?"

Kriker grinned. "We're talkin' about a little girl's life here and all you give a damn about is the money."

Guild grinned back. "I like your piety, Kriker."

"What's 'piety'?"

"You've been killing people and robbing people all over the Territory for twenty years and I try to collect a reward on you and you get all pissed up and self-righteous."

"I never killed nobody innocent."

"Somebody killed the girl's folks."

"Wasn't me." He sighed. "Anyway, later on I killed the man what done it."

"I've got half of what I wanted."

"What's that supposed to mean?"

110

"It means I've got the Bruckner brothers tied up. Now I get the money and I'll have all I wanted. I'll take the money and the brothers back to Sheriff Decker and get the reward and ride out of here."

"What about me? You don't want to take me in?"

"We're going to make a trade."

"A trade?"

"You're going to tell me where the money is, and then you're going to get on your horse and get out of here."

"What about Maundy?"

"The girl's staying so a doc can help her."

Tears came into the mountain man's eyes again, and Guild could see that his fear and hatred of docs was just as powerful in the voodoo sense as the granny woman's medicines. "The doc'll kill her! The doc'll kill her!"

But Guild was past it now with the man. He felt sorry for him and was moved by his love for the little girl, but the little girl needed a doc and Guild needed the reward money and needed to turn over the Bruckners, who'd killed Rig and young Tolliver. The one part of hunting bounty he'd never liked was that not everybody made it easy for you. Sometimes Guild saw that he was very little different from the man he was stalking, and sometimes that made things difficult indeed. But you got past it and the professional part of yourself took over and while it was not an admirable part of yourself perhaps it was a necessary part.

Kriker had put his head down and was starting to sob, and Guild said, "I'll stay here with the doc personally, Kriker. I'll be with him all the time. I'll make sure that he doesn't do anything to the girl. You understand that?"

Kriker raised his head. His eyes and nose were running and his beard was filled with mucus. "I don't want her to die, Guild. I don't want her to die."

He sounded unimaginably young and terrified, and now all Guild himself could do was put his own head down.

When he raised it, he said, "Where'd you put the money, Kriker?" He said it very softly, so softly the popping of the potbellied stove nearly covered his words.

"There's a cave on a ridge to the north of here. There's a crooked oak in front of it. The money's in there. I don't give a damn about the money no more. I just want Maundy to be all right." He stared at Guild. "You promise you won't let that doc hurt her?"

"I promise."

" 'Cause I'd find you."

"I know."

"And I'd kill you."

"I wouldn't blame you."

" 'Cause I love her."

Guild stood up and that's when somebody burst through the cabin door and said, "Somebody took the girl and knocked out the granny woman!"

Kriker made a noise Guild could equate only with a huge animal that had been badly wounded.

Guild picked up his double 10-gauge and said, "Son of a bitch. Son of a bitch."

Then they all went to Kriker's cabin.

CHAPTER FOURTEEN

"You got what you wanted, didn't you?" Kriker shouted at the priest half an hour later.

The two men stood only inches apart in the center of the cabin where the girl had lain.

The granny woman, favoring her head with a knobby hand, sat in a corner shaking her head as if she could still not believe what had taken place.

Inside the stove, wind from the chimney chased the flames in a whoosh of fire.

Three settlement men stood and watched as Kriker, still cuffed, paced back and forth in the cabin after screaming at the priest.

"You got what you wanted, you miserable son of a bitch! I wouldn't be surprised if you had something to do with it!"

The granny woman glanced up and said, softly and sorrowfully, "He didn't have nothin' to do with it, Kriker. Nothin' at all."

Kriker waved his cuffed fists in frustration and fury.

The snow was getting heavy and wetter. Guild went down the long slope of the hill, digging in his heels. By now the moon was so snowed over there was nothing but shadow and snowdrifts on the land. The only sound was the wind and, faintly, his own boots, the creak of leather and crunch of ice.

They were gone from the tree, the Bruckner brothers, just as he'd expected.

Uselessly, he bent down and picked up the rope that had bound them. He hefted it in his hands as if it had the power to impart some knowledge he vitally needed.

But he was stalling and he knew it. He just didn't want to have to see Kriker's face again. The girl gone, Kriker had become the sort of animal the human mind cannot comfortably deal with, one so lost in grief he is capable of any act at all.

Guild threw the rope down and started back up the slope, the wind knocking him to the left and then to the right, not permitting him straight passage.

He was about halfway up the hill, black sky behind the rocks and pines on the rim, when he heard a moan he first dismissed as the wind.

But the moan came again and he knew better, and now he went left on purpose, over across a sheer shine of ice coating to a jagged boulder. The closer he got, the clearer two thick black sticks became.

Then he realized that the thick black sticks were human legs.

The old Indian had crawled behind the boulder for protection from the wind. It hadn't done him much good. He had ten or twenty breaths in him and no more.

Guild raised the man's head and said, "Where's your horse?"

The Indian, parchment brown, parchment wrinkled, smelled of urine and sweat despite the cold. He said, "Lawman."

The Bruckners, of course. "Burned face?"

The Indian nodded.

Guild said, "I'm taking you to the settlement."

The Indian started to cry.

Guild threw the old man over his shoulder and started once more down the hill. The old man had the effect of anchoring Guild. The strain was greater, but the wind no longer blew Guild around.

He could feel him dying. You could tell by the coughing. The old Indian's lungs pressed against Guild's back and he could feel death come that way. In little spasms. Then there weren't any spasms at all.

Guild didn't put him down, though. He carried him the rest of the way to Kriker's cabin and then set him on the floor and everybody there looked at the dead brown man and shook their heads, and one said, "Bruckners?"

And all Guild could do was nod and stare over at Kriker, who had his face buried in the pillow where the girl's head had lain.

Guild was watching Kriker roll his face back and forth on the pillow when one of the settlement men started gagging just before he started vomiting.

Guild said to Healy the priest, "It's starting. The cholera."

Healy the priest said something he probably shouldn't have. He said, "Shit."

Guild said, "Now we've got to wait for two things."

"What's that?" Healy said.

"Word from the Bruckners on how they want to make the trade for the girl."

"And?"

Guild nodded to the two men helping the sick man out of the door. "And the cholera to start. You know how it goes. Half this settlement could be dead by tomorrow night."

This time the priest responded more appropriately. He said, "My God."

CHAPTER FIFTEEN

Once there had been a city named Yankton, and it had been a fine city with electric lights that glowed in the darkness and fine shiny carriages pulled by fine shiny horses and a park where a calliope could be heard on summer nights and a band shell where a hundred musicians played music so beautiful that even the stars seemed to brighten.

Once there had been a two-story house with the kind of exterior decoration called gingerbread (which the girl always giggled at hearing, thinking of gingerbread as something little girls such as herself ate as special treats). Once there had also been a sunny room where a gray cat named Naomi stretched in the sunlight and where a plump pink doll named Estelle watched everything that went on in the room with her blue button eyes. Maundy was the only one in the world who knew that Estelle could talk; she had decided it would be best for all concerned to keep Estelle's abilities a secret.

Once there had been a tall, handsome father given to three-piece suits and working late at his law office, and once there had been a short, pretty mother given to holding Maundy on her knee and reading to her stories by a man named Sir Walter Scott and a woman named Louisa May Alcott. Maundy liked especially Louisa May.

Then one summer there had been a stage trip (Father having said, "There's no direct train route there," and then cursing as always the territorial government for its inadequacies) to see Cousin Daniel on his farm.

And that's when it happened — the frightened shout of the stagecoach driver, the pounding of hooves coming from the surrounding woods, and then the quick sharp ear-hurting sound of gunfire, and the tart gray smell of it, too.

The robbers had made Father, Mother, and herself step down from the stage and raise their hands the way people had to in the melodramas her parents liked to attend, and then for no reason two of the robbers simply started shooting and —

— and she could remember nothing else about that period of her life.

Occasionally she would try to reconstruct

the rest of what had happened that day, but something in her mind would not let the images form.

The gunfire . . . and Father screaming and Mother leaning down to him and screaming herself and . . .

Then there was the man named Kriker. He had a beard like a bear's and a belly like a bison's, and he wore hide for clothes instead of cotton or flannel, and when he spoke he talked the way the poor people of Yankton did, with "ain'ts" and "ain't a gonnas" and all those other things that Miss Meister always said made her "positively cringe."

Kriker was one of the four robbers, but he hadn't done any of the shooting. In fact, he shouted for the shooting to stop, but by then it had been too late.

Kriker took her back to the settlement then and began the long process of trying to get her to talk. That was the funny thing about Kriker. You wouldn't think a man who wore hides and who shunned civilized things would have such patience or sweetness or gentleness, but he did. Those qualities glowed in his eyes and gentled his tongue, and she had learned quickly enough not to be afraid of him.

But still she couldn't talk.

121

Green summers and white winters came and went, and she found herself becoming part of the settlement itself, doing chores and picking wild flowers and learning how squirrels and raccoons were skinned for stew meat and how milk snakes were ugly but could not hurt you and how rattlesnakes were pretty in their way but could kill you.

Her hair grew long and her limbs grew longer. One day Kriker brought from town a doll that resembled Estelle not in the least, but a doll she loved in as peculiar a way as she loved Kriker.

But still she could not talk.

The granny woman spent hours with her, fumbling with herbs and mice bones and rabbit pelts, but still she could not talk.

The priest spent hours with her, fumbling with holy water and incense and fine blue swaths of cloth, but still she could not talk.

Kriker spent hours with her, holding her in his lap there in the rocker as birds sang softly in the purple dusk, but still she could not talk.

She wanted to talk, of course, and tried to talk, and sounds welled in her throat and filled her mouth, but they were not words, just sounds, and so she did not, no matter how she tried, talk.

And the settlement people came to accept

this, shaping the air with gestures that said "Thank you" or "Isn't it a beautiful day?" or "Would you like to run in the woods?" or "Is it time to fill your belly?"

There had been a time when she could talk — when, indeed, Father at the Sunday table filled with roast beef and chocolate cake had called her his "little chatterbox" — but words now were some secret lost seemingly forever.

Forever.

She dreamed of these things as she lay in the corner of the line shack where the two men who'd taken her from the village had placed her.

She dreamed of these things and of a visit to St. Loo and of a train trip east to New York and of how her mother had said that someday Maundy would have her own children and of how Father smelled after shaving, clean and spicy, and how her cat had stretched so gray and beautiful in the sunlight on the white spread of her bed.

She dreamed of these things as she lay there dying.

"He won't kill you."
"He sure will."
"We've got the girl."

"You know what he's like."

"I know what he's like, but I also know we got the girl." Thomas Bruckner paused. "You put a piece of that white sheet on your carbine and you ride into that settlement and you ask to see Kriker."

"I wouldn't even get that far."

"I wouldn't send you if I thought he'd kill you." James Bruckner shook his head. "You can just imagine what he'll be like now."

"I can also imagine that robbery money. It's part ours, anyway."

James Bruckner looked around the line shack. When the railroads had cut through the timber paralleling the frozen river below, they'd needed temporary facilities for materials and bosses. Shacks such as these were dotted all over the Territory. They smelled of wood and creosote and damp earth. The grave probably would not smell much different. In the summer dogs and rats and cats and snakes slept in them, and termites and worms feasted on them. But now it was too cold for anything except human beings.

When the girl moaned, James Bruckner looked over at her. He'd set a match to a kerosene lantern twenty minutes ago, and now the lantern light showed that her lips were so dry from fever they'd started to crack and bleed.

James said, "She better not die."

"She won't die."

"I could barely feel her pulse."

"She won't die."

"He'd hunt us down if she did. There wouldn't be anyplace we could go without him findin' us."

"You just take that piece of sheet and the carbine and the horse and you ride into that settlement and you tell him if he gives us the money, then an hour later he's got the girl."

"I still say he'll kill me."

"You're just like Ma."

"Don't say nothin' against Ma."

"I ain't," Thomas Bruckner said, knowing how sensitive a subject Ma was with James. "I just mean you always look on the dark side."

"Sometimes that seems like the only side there is."

"I look on the bright side."

"You don't have my face."

"You know that woman in St. Loo. She liked you that time."

"That's 'cause she was crippled and she knew what it was like havin' people stare at you all the time."

"She said she wanted to marry you, didn't she?"

"Yeah, but I saw how she always looked at those other guys. The ones without faces like mine. I saw how she looked at them."

The girl moaned again.

"You better be headin' out, James. You better be headin' out right away."

"He's gonna shoot me, Thomas. He's gonna shoot me for sure."

But Thomas wasn't listening. He went over and tore off a piece of the soiled sheet on which the girl lay on the rusted springs that had once been a bed. He took the white rag and tied it to the cold steel barrel of the carbine and then he handed it back to James.

"I love you, James. I surely do."

Thomas leaned over and kissed him on the cheek. The burned cheek. "I'm sorry for the way I am sometimes. But I do try to be a good brother, James. A true one."

Thomas always did this whenever James wavered about doing a particularly dangerous job. A brotherly kiss and then kind words.

But he sent James out anyway, of course, and without hesitation at all.

Just the way that day, so long ago now yet so perfectly frozen in James's mind, when

Thomas had splashed the kerosene on him and then tossed the match.

Just the same way.

CHAPTER SIXTEEN

Three had died in the past half hour. The cholera, as cholera always did, struck swiftly. You got stomach cramps that literally threw you around and then you began vomiting and then your fever shot up and then you were dead. Sometimes all this could transpire within three hours, start to finish, and you'd be dead. In the Territory there was nothing like it. Nothing.

Guild sat in the cabin where the girl had been. Kriker, still cuffed, sat in the chair across from him. Guild had his double 10-gauge in his lap.

He said to Kriker, "Why not take the drink I offered?"

"I need my mind clear."

"I'm going to handle the Bruckners, Kriker. Not you."

Kriker, curiously reserved the past twenty minutes, said, "You owe me that at least. For the little girl's sake."

They stared at each other and then Guild said, "Maybe you're right, Kriker. Maybe I do owe you that."

"I don't know many men who'd steal a little girl."

"I guess I don't, either."

"You should have seen her with this blue hair ribbon I bought her last spring."

"Pretty, I'll bet."

"Real pretty." Pause. "She could die, she's so sick."

"She won't die, Kriker. We'll get her back. Just have some whiskey. We'll hear from them soon."

Kriker said, his eyes tearing up again, "You ever have children?"

"No."

"Then you don't know what I mean."

"I know what you mean, Kriker. I know just what you mean." Guild thought about the little girl. He'd been tracking a man to a cabin and he'd seen a rifle glint inside the door and he'd raised his gun instinctively and fired. Then he'd seen that the person with the rifle had been a little girl. The wanted man had been her father, who had left her behind. The girl died right in front of Guild, right in the doorway. All he could do was watch, the way the blood bloomed on her chest, and then the soft clear childish tears there at the quick last. There'd been great outrage and a trial, but he had been found innocent although not once had he ever felt innocent. Which was why, even as a Lutheran, he so often went to Catholic church and confession. To rid his mind of her image, the little girl dying there before the cabin, the scent of pines ridiculously sweet that day, the sky ridiculously blue.

"You aren't going to have that whiskey, I am," Guild said and got up and crossed the cabin floor and poured himself some bourbon. He had had maybe two fingers when the cabin door swung open and with it came icy snow and wind that cut knife sharp.

Father Healy stood there, dazed. "Half the settlement's down with cholera. Half the settlement." He nodded to Guild. "You have any idea what we can do?"

"All we can do is wait till the girl gets back with the doc."

Father Healy said, almost to himself, "Maybe this is my fault."

"What?" Guild said.

Then Father Healy shook the thought away and said, "You haven't heard from the Bruckners yet?"

"No."

The priest nodded to Kriker. "How's he?"

"Not much better."

The priest went over to Kriker and said, "The girl's going to be all right. I'm sure she is."

Kriker's rage was back. "You ain't no priest so don't go around makin' like one! Just get out of this cabin and leave me alone!"

Guild put his hand on the priest's shoulder and pulled him away from Kriker, leading him to the door and outside.

They stood in the wind and the ice and the silver roaring night. It was like being on a very high mountain in the blizzard season.

Guild said, "What'd you mean back there when you said it was your fault?"

Father Healy, exhausted looking, said, "Because I don't have faith. Because, like Kriker said, I'm not really a priest. And that's what we need now. A real doc and a real priest. Otherwise —" He shook his head again, talking loud into the voice-taking wind. "You see, Mr. Guild, back in Chicago I —"

Guild stopped him. "I remember the poster on you."

"Poster?"

"Wanted poster. In all the law offices. A bounty man has to have a good memory for such things. You're wanted for killing another sharp."

"I didn't kill him. My partner did. I wasn't even there. I just came out into the alley later and saw him on the ground there and then somebody else came and saw me and started shouting and — and I got blamed. So I ran and eventually I came here." He pointed to the semicircle of cabins seen through the haze of snow. "They're good people, Guild. They've started life over and they're raising families and — and now this." He stared at Guild again. "They need a doc and a priest."

"There's a lot of different ways to be a priest, Healy," Guild said. "Best one I ever knew smelled of beer half the time and had wooden teeth and couldn't pronounce his Latin. But he was damn good when you needed comfort, and that's all these people need now. Comfort. That's what being a priest is, Healy, and that's all it is."

He had just finished speaking when he saw a lone rider on a grulla coming down the perilous slope from the north. The grulla slipped every few steps. The rider held his carbine high, like an Indian lance. Attached to it was a piece of white cloth. The rider was James Bruckner.

He kept shouting, "Don't shoot! Don't shoot!"

Guild had never wanted to kill a man so badly in his life.

CHAPTER SEVENTEEN

He put the double 10-gauge directly into James Bruckner's face and said, "Get down."

Bruckner said, "You're not going to kill me, are you, Mr. Guild?"

"I said get down."

With the wind, you could scarcely hear their voices. You could see how the grulla was exhausted and frightened from the trip. Snow as light as dust blew over them.

James Bruckner said, "Please don't kill me, Mr. Guild."

Guild slammed the barrel of the double 10-gauge against Bruckner's temple. Bruckner jolted and screamed. Guild had hit him very hard.

Bruckner's own weapon looked like a toy with the white rag tied to its end. He climbed down from the grulla.

Guild switched hands with the double 10-gauge. He wanted his right free.

He hit James Bruckner in the mouth and then in the ribs and then in the mouth again. When Bruckner dropped to his knees, Guild kicked him in the jaw.

Bruckner tumbled over backward and lay sprawled on the ice.

Father Healy came up from behind Guild and said, "Is there any call for that?"

"I need to be alone with him, Father." Then, hearing how harsh his voice was, he turned sideways to the priest and said, "Please."

"I'm asking you not to hit him anymore."

Guild looked at the priest for a long moment and then nodded. "I won't hit him anymore."

The priest nodded and went away.

Guild dropped to his knees and scooped up handfuls of snow and threw them on James Bruckner's burned face.

When Bruckner came to, Guild slapped him once viciously, then remembered what he'd promised the priest.

Bruckner looked almost surprised that Guild had stopped with just a slap.

Then Guild jerked the other man to his feet by the lapels and dragged him into the central cabin where the meeting had been.

He did not want Bruckner in the same cabin with Kriker. He knew what that would

135

do to Kriker.

He said, "Where's the girl?"

"He just wants the money."

"You didn't answer my question."

James Bruckner, bruised badly from Guild's fist and foot, shook his burned face sorrowfully. "Either way I turn, Mr. Guild, somebody's gonna be out for me. If I tell you where he is, he'll kill me. If I don't tell you where he is, you're gonna be mad."

"She all right?"

Bruckner dropped his eyes. "Thomas says she is."

"You don't think so?"

"She's real sick."

"What's Thomas want to do?"

"He wants me to go with you and get the money and then he wants you to give me the money and then we'll turn over the girl."

"I want the girl first."

"He says no, Thomas does."

"You really think I'd trust you or your brother to turn her over?"

"What would we want with her?"

"Why'd you kill Rig and Tolliver?"

"We didn't."

"You're a liar."

He forgot about his agreement with the priest. He caught James Bruckner on the side of the head, where the right sort of punch would daze him and make him nauseated. Then he kicked him twice quickly in the shins and then he slapped him again.

James Bruckner started crying.

"Why'd you kill Rig and Tolliver?"

"I didn't. Thomas did."

"Why did Thomas kill Rig and Tolliver?"

"He wanted all the shares of the money plus he was afraid they'd tell."

"Tell Decker?"

"Yes. The Territory's gettin' smaller. You get a rep for doublin' as a lawman and a bank robber and —" He shook his head sorrowfully again.

Guild took his double 10-gauge and said, "I'm going back with you."

"What?"

"We're not going to get the money. We're going to get the girl and your brother."

"You don't know Thomas."

"What's that mean?"

"He'd kill her. He'd kill that little girl."

Guild stared at him. "You know what you're saying about your own brother?"

"I know."

"That he'd kill a little child."

"Yes."

"Your own brother?"

"It's how he is, Mr. Guild."

Guild, sensing James Bruckner was probably telling the truth, said, "Son of a bitch."

"What?"

"Don't talk."

"What?"

Guild, whirling on him, said, "I said don't talk. You understand? Don't talk."

James Bruckner dropped his head the way a chastised child would.

Guild paced and thought through things well as he could. He was tired and cold, and he kept thinking of the little girl. By now, of course, he was thinking crazy thoughts. If he could save the life of this little girl, then that would somehow lessen the terrible thing he had done to the other little girl.

He had to save this little girl. Had to.

He said, "We're going to go get the money, you and me, and then you're going to take it back to your brother."

James Bruckner said, "It's the best way, Mr. Guild. Given how Thomas is and all. I don't want no little girl to be hurt, either."

"If you're so different from your brother, why do you stay with him?"

"Look at my face," James Bruckner said. "Who else'd have me?"

■ ■ ■ ■

Ten minutes later, Guild stood in Kriker's cabin. The man lay on the cot staring at the ceiling. He had a rosary entwined in his fingers. The handcuffs were still on him. Now Guild handcuffed his ankles as well. He didn't want Kriker getting crazy and spoiling Guild's plan. Kriker hardly seemed to notice the cuffs on his hands. His fingers just kept working the rosary and his wet mouth kept praying big silent words and his eyes kept staring with a certain fixated madness at the cabin ceiling.

Guild said, "What's the easiest way to get to that cave?"

Kriker said, "There was gunfire awhile ago. Who was that?"

"Just me. I thought I saw something."

"There any word on Maundy yet?"

"No."

"You haven't heard from the Bruckners?"

Guild considered telling him, then decided he wouldn't be doing Kriker any favors. "No."

"God." Kriker sounded on the verge of tears again.

"It helps, doesn't it, to pray?"

"Yes."

139

"You just keep praying."

Kriker had gone back to staring at the ceiling. He didn't say anything now. He looked utterly beyond words.

Guild went back to the cabin where he'd tied James Bruckner to a chair.

On the way the priest stopped him. "Two more."

"Dead?"

"Yes."

Guild said, "In St. Loo four hundred died in one afternoon." Then he nodded to the semicircle of cabins. "You know what they need, Father. Comfort."

The priest nodded and hurried on to the next cabin.

CHAPTER EIGHTEEN

Guild took strips of hide and lashed James Bruckner to his saddlehorn, and then Guild swung up on his own horse and they set off to find the cave.

Both men wore bandannas over their faces and both men kept their heads down. Guild estimated the temperature now at close to zero. Purchase anywhere was difficult for the horses. If there was a trail it had been covered by drifting snow hours earlier. Despite gloves he felt the cold in his fingers especially and in his toes even though he wore $5.50-a-dozen lumberman's socks from a Sears store in Yankton.

As they rode, Guild tried to ease his mind from the girl by thinking of a tent-show speech he'd heard once about the Ice Age, how more than a quarter of the planet had been covered with impenetrable sheets of ice, and how two million years later glaciers formed such places as Yosemite Valley, and how right here in the Territory itself there had been an immense glacial lake called Lake Agassiz. When he thought of the things the professor had said that day in his fine, barking politician's voice, it was easy enough to imagine that another such age had befallen the planet and that the only two people left were himself and Bruckner, tight reining their ice-flanked horses through the eternal night.

He thought of these things as the wind whipped and the plains before them resembled a white tundra with silver dust demons and a sudden moon gazing down on them like the callous eye of a pitiless god. Everywhere you saw small black dots and knew they were animals — squirrels and raccoons and possums — that had frozen in the remorseless night. The only touch of ugly splendor anywhere was in the branches of the dead trees, silvered with ice and glinting like jewelry.

Twice Bruckner's horse slipped and pitched, and both times Bruckner, lashed to the saddle-horn, slammed his head against the unyielding ground. The second time blood began to trickle from his nose. Guild blotted at it with the man's bandanna but he did not cut him free. The second time, getting the horse up was especially difficult, the animal biting Guild's hand hard enough to draw a line of blood beneath the fabric of the glove. After a quick curse at the animal, Guild then reached over and patted the horse. Guild did not blame him for resenting the task they'd set for him. Guild would have bitten his captor, too.

So finally they continued on their way, three hours after leaving the settlement, the wind, if anything, fiercer, the cold more unremitting.

There would be no end to this night, Guild thought, and during it they would fall to the white ground beneath the silver dust devils and the pitiless eye of the moon and become stiff and black like the dead possums and squirrels strewn across the tundra.

A few times Father Healy wondered if he wasn't feeling feverish himself, but then he decided, no, it was only his imagination. His mother in Chicago had always said he'd been blessed with two things: "a face the girls will love and an imagination that'll someday sure and get you in trouble."

Father Healy had spent the last two hours isolating those who showed any symptoms of the disease in the big central cabin. There were not enough cots to go around so the priest and the granny woman, who had reluctantly agreed to help him (she having no more faith in the God he espoused than he did in her remedies), spread out woolen blankets and pillows on the floor and then began to minister to the people one by one.

The smells of vomit and sweat were overpowering. Stomach cramps got so bad in people that they jerked about on the floor as if possessed. Every few moments somebody called out for water. But the eyes were worst. Newspaper accounts invariably described choleric eyes as "sinking." What they meant was that the eyes became those of dead people — a milky white without expression.

Outside the cabin door, huddled under the overhang, family members of the sick people waited word, which too often now came when a pair of burly men would be quietly summoned by Father Healy. The men would come in, wrap the corpse in its woolen blanket, and then take it outside, to put it in the communal barn. Their trek would be accompanied by the cries and screams of the children and spouses who had loved the man or woman. Twice the burly men had carried out small children wrapped in the coarse woolen blankets, and that was the worst, of course, children. The men put them in a special place in the barn, away from the others, and one of the men, after the second child, went over to a wall and began kicking it savagely, until a huge hole was rent into the side of the barn. This calmed him and he went back to waiting for another summons from the priest. All he could hope was that the next summons would not be for a child.

At one point Father Healy had to go to the cabin of a couple whose child had just died. The boy had been their only child.

When he entered, he found them sitting apart from each other, some terrible isolation imposed on them, as if the grief of their loss could not be shared any more than their own deaths would be shared in the final moments. They were alone, utterly and irretrievably alone.

He went in, beads in his soft hands, and said, "He's with the Lord now."

"Stan, he has his gun," the woman said, and at first Father Healy did not understand her meaning.

Then he saw that the husband sat on the edge of the cot with his Sharps positioned in such a way that he could easily put it in his mouth. This certainly was not unheard of in the Territory. Disease, drought, hard luck in the hills when gold had been promised but never appeared — man was the only animal who resorted to taking his own life, and this seemed at different times to Father Healy both a blessing and a curse.

"He don't want to live," the woman said. The cabin was in shadows because of the low-turned kerosene lamp, and the woman's words filled the priest's ears and he knew what she was saying — in effect, he doesn't want to live and it's up to you to change his mind.

As always, Healy turned almost instinctively to some sense of order and justice in the universe — to what others called God. How many nights had he lain in his solitary bed trying to summon up faith in such a deity, but always there was just the darkness and the silence. It seemed the most you could hope for was song in the wine and laughter in the dungeon, and that it was a world of utter chance, and when chance came against you, you were obliterated, literally, becoming an element of the cosmic darkness itself.

But then he remembered what the bounty man Guild had said about people needing comfort, and he knew then that Guild was right. Even if it was all a fake, this pretense of order and meaning, then it was a necessary fake and an ennobling one.

He said to Stan, gently as he could, "Next

summer would be a good time for a child, Stan."

Stan said nothing.

"You told me once how you were planning on having another one," the priest said.

Still, Stan said nothing.

"Think of when the grass is green again and the sky is blue and there's trout in the stream where we fished that time. Mae here would love to have you another child, wouldn't you, Mae?"

And Mae flew to her husband then, seeing the opportunity the priest had given her, huddling against her husband, crying and helping him to cry, too, at the bitter death of their six-year-old.

"She's been a good wife to you, Stan," Father Healy said. "If you killed yourself, think what you'd be doing to Mae."

And as he began to cry full now, the hard and racking and reluctant way a man cries, the priest who was not after all a priest stepped forward softly in the shadows and took from the aggrieved man the Sharps.

Stan's fingers held the gun only briefly, then released it. "She loves you, Stan," said the priest who was not after all a priest. "She loves you."

And then Father Healy left, going back to the cabin to find the two burly men, and he passed a sobbing group of women and children carrying out another wool-wrapped corpse.

Near dawn they found it.

The place was just as Kriker had described — the trees in the exact formation, though bent now from wind and ice, the cave mouth oval-shaped with a jagged overhang that dipped down.

When he dismounted, Guild saw that his horse was beginning to shudder from exertion and the cold. From his jacket pocket, Guild took a handful of oats and held them up to the animal's mouth. Then he went over and fed Bruckner's grulla.

He said, "I'm going in the cave and get the money." He waved the double 10-gauge at the tundra before them. Faint down the sky came ragged streaks of yellow and pink dawn. The round moon now had a flat look the darker sky had given dimension. "You can take off if you want to, Bruckner, but if anything happens to your horse, he'll take you down with him."

For emphasis, Guild rapped the handcuffs attached to the saddlehorn.

Bruckner said, "I won't be goin' nowhere." He sounded sullen and young, and even though Guild felt sorry for the man and what his burned face must have done to him, he also hated him for going along with his brother's blackmail plan.

Guild walked up to the cave entrance, his boots crunching through snow that snapped like glass.

He had just ducked under the overhang and started inside when he heard the unmistakable low rumble of a timber wolf.

He saw the wolf's eyes glowing there in the darkness and then he took a very deep breath.

He sensed that the animal — frozen and afraid — might do what very few wolves ever did, despite the stories surrounding them.

The wolf might attack.

"You don't talk much."

Nothing.

"You scared?"

Nothing.

"I got no reason to hurt you. There's no reason to be scared."

She had come awake so abruptly, color coming back to her cheeks and eyes, that it had been like a dead person resurrecting. Thomas Bruckner thought of his Bible lesson about Lazarus.

He said, "You want some water?"

She nodded. Her face had an eerie luminous quality, especially her gaze. It made Bruckner uncomfortable and he wanted to tell her to quit looking at him, but he realized it would only make him sound crazy — or somehow afraid of her — and it wouldn't do to have a small girl think you were afraid of her.

He got her water from the canteen and held her head up and helped her drink and then eased her back on her blankets.

He put a hand to her cheek. "Whoo," he said. Then he stared at her. "Ain't you curious what I was sayin' 'Whoo' about?"

She fell into her unnerving silence again.

"I was sayin' 'Whoo' about your cheek. You're still burnin' up."

He plunked himself down next to her cot and huddled into his clothes. The windows rattled and the roof was like to tear off the way it sounded in the wind. Flame fluttered in the kerosene lamp and far distant you could hear animals — cows most likely — down along the rough line of barbed wire.

He did not like the feeling of isolation that had suddenly overtaken him. He felt vulnerable. He needed to talk.

If only to a small girl who couldn't, or wouldn't, talk back.

"I suppose you think I'm a real baddie."

Nothing.

"What with me stealin' you and all."

Nothing.

"But I only done it 'cause I figured Kriker'd give us the money and then we could leave." He paused and thought about rolling a cigarette and then thought, no, he would have to take off his gloves and dig deep in the shirt beneath his sweater and sheepskin and —

"You seen my brother's face?" By now he no longer expected the girl to say anything. He just wanted to hear his own voice here above the wind. "I did that to him. When we was kids. It was only a joke, but I don't think deep down he believes that." He paused once more to look back at the girl. Her eyes were open, but they were beginning to take on the same faded quality as before. He glanced around at the line shack. In the summer, after a hard ten hours' work in the sun, it probably would have been nice to come back here and roll cigarettes and drink local wine and listen to the summer night. He had begun thinking about summer now. It helped cut down the wind and the sound of isolation. "We get the money now, I'm takin' my brother to California, and I'm gonna buy him new clothes and give him a right nice time." Pause. "You

know, sort of make things up to him. Then
—" He shook his head, about to say something he'd needed to say for years. "Then
I'm gonna tell him good-bye. He's got to
find his own life and I got to find mine. With
his face and all —" He shook his head
again. "Well, he ain't real easy to find
friends for and I guess I kind of resent it
and I take advantage of him and —" He
exhaled as if he had just finished some very
difficult task. "He'll be all right. On his own,
I mean. I'll give him a good share of the
money — ten percent, I figure — and buy
him a fresh horse in addition to the clothes
and" — he shrugged — "and then I won't
have to worry about him no more."

He sounded very satisfied suddenly, as if
the problem that had been so long burden-
ing him had resolved itself with an ease so
miraculous he could not quite believe it.

He said, "You want some more water?"

But he was turned away from her and then
he remembered that the girl didn't speak.
Or wouldn't.

So he turned around and looked at her
and said, "You want some water?"

And the wind — it had never sounded
more like alien song.

And the fragile line shack — it had never
sounded more like it was being ripped apart.

And Thomas William Bruckner, he had never felt more like all the men he'd killed had come back for him. He'd had dreams of that many times, and now he could see the men as in the stories of Edgar Allan Poe the chautauqua speakers so liked to read — dead and coming back for him.

"You want some more water?" he said again.

But then the wind was up again, and as he gazed down on her he realized that there had been some subtle shift in the angle of her repose and that she looked — poor little girl who reminded him suddenly of one of his many sisters back on the farm — she looked different somehow.

He lifted the canteen and started to bring it close to her parched mouth.

And then he realized why she struck him as having changed, realized why she did not look to be exactly the same little girl his brother had earlier taken from the settlement.

Because she was no longer the same little girl.

In fact, she was no little girl at all.

She was nothing.

She was dead.

CHAPTER NINETEEN

Guild had just struck a Telegraph sulfur match against a dry jut of rock on the roof of the cave when the wolf lunged.

Two quick impressions: the cave was shallow and narrow. Near the back was a pile of small rocks, once more just as Kriker had described, beneath which he would find the bank robbery money.

The second impression was that of the wolf itself. In addition to the powerful teeth revealed as the mouth pulled back in a growl, in addition to the bushy tail and the enormous round pupils of the eyes, in addition to the yellow-gray fur and the white markings on the feet — in addition to all these he saw the dried blood on the side of the wolf, exposing a white glimpse of rib cage.

Something had attacked the wolf earlier and the wolf had crawled here to the cave, using it as a lair in the frozen night, and now intruders had come and —

Which explained why a creature who rarely attacked anything other than small prairie animals and birds — except in packs, when they were then bold enough to go after sheep and bison — would lunge at him now.

Guild had just time to drop to one knee and level the double 10-gauge.

But the wolf surprised him by diving over Guild's shoulder and going straight out of the cave and then jumping up on the grulla holding James Bruckner.

The wolf moved with a blind savagery that Guild could not quite grasp.

Before Guild had time to respond, the wolf had dug its powerful teeth into the side of the grulla and had ripped away a large chunk of bloody flesh.

The animal reared up, crying out above the wind as the wolf continued to leap and rend, even managing to tear away more flesh as the grulla was up on its rears.

Now James Bruckner's screams joined the grulla's. Handcuffed to the saddlehorn, Bruckner clung helplessly to the back of the grulla, the wolf beginning now to snap at Bruckner's legs.

Guild dropped to one knee again and fired.

He got the wolf in the side of the head, a large hole appearing where there had been an eye and the beginnings of a snout.

Then, just to be safe, he sent another one through the wolf's chest.

The yellow-gray animal flopped over on the snow. A silver dust devil whirling up off the tundra began immediately to cover it in white.

The grulla, bleeding badly from the wolf's attack, had now fallen over on its side, its legs kicking uselessly in pain, as if it were going somewhere.

James Bruckner was crying.

Guild got down and took out his handcuff key and got Bruckner separated from the saddle and then yanked the man away from the grulla.

Bruckner said, "What you gonna do, Mr. Guild?" But he saw very well what Guild was going to do.

Guild got the double 10-gauge ready.

"You got to do it, Mr. Guild?"

"Look at him," Guild said. "You think I like it any better than you do?"

"Can I turn around?"

"I don't care."

"Thomas, he says I'm a coward."

"You want me to tell you what Thomas is?"

"I guess I already know that." Pause. The grulla was shrieking, writhing, massive and dying on the white. Red snow formed an ever-widening pool.

"You don't mind, then?" James asked.

"I want to do it fast. For the horse's sake." He stared at James. James stared at the animal. You could see James was scared and heartsick for the horse. Guild said softly, "You can turn around, James. No sense in you watchin'."

"You gonna watch?"

"I'm gonna close my eyes. Otherwise I couldn't do it."

"Poor goddamn thing."

"Yes," Guild said softly. "Poor goddamned thing."

James Bruckner turned around and Guild shot the grulla in the head.

When he turned back to Bruckner, Guild saw that the man was crying again. Guild went over and stood in front of him in the wind, hearing its mordant eternal sound.

James Bruckner tried to hide the fact that he was crying, but he wasn't doing a very good job of it. He said, "Sometimes I like horses a lot better than I do people."

Guild smiled. "You know something, Bruckner?"

"What?"

"So do I."

Then Guild got Bruckner up on his horse and handcuffed him to the saddlehorn, and then Guild went in and got the bank robbery money.

There were two satchels of it and there was plenty enough, green and crisp as it was, to kill people over if that was your inclination.

He went back out and took the reins of the horse and started the trek back to the settlement, James Bruckner snuffling from what had happened to the horse.

Kriker sat in the corner of the cabin, watching as the granny woman poured him coffee from a tin pot. The priest had asked her to stop in and see how Kriker was doing.

Kriker said, "Any more die?"

"Not in the last two hours," She nodded to the window. A light blue sky filled the windows. "The father says maybe the worst of it's over."

"He doesn't know nothin' about it."

The granny woman handed him the coffee. "You shouldn't hate him so much, Kriker. He ain't no better or no worse than anybody else in the settlement."

"He ain't a priest."

She glared at him. "Who's to say who is a

priest and who ain't a priest? Just 'cause you got a piece of paper don't mean nothin'. That ain't what bein' a priest is about."

Even to himself, Kriker smelled. Ordinarily, at such times, he would haul water, heat it, fill a tub, and then sit in there with a cigar while somebody sat nearby to read a newspaper to him. Reading was beyond Kriker, but listening wasn't. He had always imagined the day when the girl could read to him.

Kriker said, "I need your help, granny woman."

"With what?"

"I think you know."

She averted his eyes. "I told Father Healy I'd come in and look in on you. I better be leavin'."

"They took the girl."

"I know."

"I want to go get her."

"The bounty man's goin' to do that."

Kriker paused. "You and me, we been friends a long time."

"I'll grant you that, Kriker. But the settlement's — changed."

"That why you're so trustin' of the priest?"

"You keep your tongue off him, Kriker."

Kriker sighed, held up his hands. The handcuffs had bit into his flesh enough that small tears of blood had appeared along the bone of his wrists.

"There's a saw in the shed out back," he said.

"He'd know who done it, the bounty man would. Then I'd be in trouble."

"I jus' want to go get the girl from the Bruckners and then I want to light out of here." He paused. "You know what's gonna happen to me if the bounty man gets the girl and the money back, don't you?"

"What?"

"He's gonna take me in and they're gonna hang me."

"You didn't kill nobody in that robbery."

"No, but I had to kill people before and they're gonna extradite me and then they're gonna hang me."

"I can't do it, Kriker."

"Her and me, you don't know how good we could have it livin' in California. I could get her the schoolin' she needs, and I'd get me a job in some factory somewhere, and it could be real good for both of us. Then you and the priest, you'd have the settlement here and you could run it any way you wanted to."

Obviously the granny woman was being swept up in his words. Despite her age lines, she had the look of a child fascinated by a clever uncle.

The granny woman said, "She's your curse."

"Who?"

"The girl."

"My curse?"

"Sure. If it wasn't for her, you could do just what I told you yesterday — ride out of here clean and fast."

"She's my daughter."

"She ain't your daughter."

"As good as."

"As good as don't make her your daughter."

"You don't like her?"

The granny woman shrugged. "You was a good leader for the settlement till you brought her here. Then you started to change. It was gradual, but you started to change. All you cared about was her. The priest, he's been helpin' people more'n you have."

"I'm sick of hearin' about the priest."

She looked at his handcuffs. "I can't help you, Kriker."

"Maybe they're hurtin' her."

"I know you love her, Kriker, but you got to calm down for your own sake. You look wild. Crazy." She went over and picked up a bottle of cheap whiskey. "Why don't you have some of this in your coffee?"

"I need a clear head."

Gently, the granny woman went over and put a hand on Kriker's shoulder. "They ain't hurtin' her, Kriker."

"You sure?"

"I'm sure. They wouldn't have no call to."

"They took her, didn't they?"

"They took her, but they ain't got no call to hurt her."

He raised his head to her, his usual ferocity lessened somewhat by his worry and the fact that he had not slept. "You could go get the saw, granny woman."

"No," she said, "no, I couldn't."

CHAPTER TWENTY

Ten minutes after he finished listening to the girl, Sheriff Decker picked up his favorite shotgun, pulled on his sheepskin, and then began walking up and down the board sidewalks of the town, handpicking the men he wanted to form the posse.

It took half an hour for the liveryman to get the eight horses ready, half an hour to kiss eight wives and twenty-three children good-bye, and half an hour to make sure that an adequate supply of warm clothing and ammunition was being brought along.

Posses were still an exciting sight in the Territory, so by the time the nine men left, a crowd had gathered in front of McBride's General Store, standing in the very sunny day in the very white snow, waving good-bye to the nine men as if they were marching off to a grand and romantic war.

None of the men's wives or children had any such notions, of course. They knew bet-

163

ter. They knew exactly what their husbands and fathers were getting into because they were not lawmen or mean men or even men particularly adept with firearms. They were instead men from the mercantile and men from the insurance company and men from the telegraph company and men from the bicycle shop and men from the barbershop. Several of them hadn't wanted to go at all but knew what young and well-educated Sheriff Decker could be like when he started in on such topics as civic responsibility (it must have been those law courses he'd taken up in Yankton that had caused him to carry on so) and how a Territory town must show the world the measure of its civilization by defending that civilization at gunpoint if necessary.

Decker rode in front on a fast sleek roan. It was beautiful as its muscles pulled and rippled in the sunlight. Not a man had mentioned the fact that what they were really doing this morning was making up for Decker's mistaken faith in the Bruckner brothers. He had spent many hours arguing to the city council that such men were needed and that, within limits, they could be trusted. Now the bounty man Guild had proved otherwise, but if the lawman Decker was the least bit ashamed, he certainly didn't show it.

Next to Decker rode the doc, a tall slender man bundled up in an Alaska-style parka with his black bag lashed to his saddle. Burmeister, his name was. He'd been one of the city councilmen Decker had always argued with over the Bruckner brothers. You had to know Burmeister well enough to notice the faint satisfied smile on his thin pale lips this morning. The Territory was becoming infested with smart-aleck young people who studied all sorts of things up in Yankton, including law and medicine, and then swaggered around the Territory acting as if they knew something you didn't. Dr. Herman Burmeister was never unhappy to see such upstarts proved wrong.

There was no snow and the sky was blue as a painting and there was no wind at all, and so they rode on fast as they could, nine men from town in the blinding white beauty of the day.

She had started to smell, so Thomas Bruckner took the little girl and wrapped her tight in the blanket and then carried her outside and placed her next to the cabin.

He was just religious enough that he considered it only fitting to say a prayer over her, and so he said a few proper words, or at least burial words, as he remembered them from all the tough Territory towns where he and his brother had roamed over the years. Then he took a shovel and covered her with enough snow so that wandering animals would leave her alone.

Because he still needed the girl.

She was dead, but in one way her part in all this had just begun.

Then he went back in the cabin and fell to cleaning his rifle and his pistol.

He kept checking his watch.

His brother should be along anytime now. Any time.

The man grabbed at Father Healy's hand and said, "Back in Ohio, Father, I used to be a Catholic."

"I see."

"I want you to hear my confession."

"I —"

Father Healy had been going to say, "I can't do that. I'm not a priest." But the man before him on the cot in the big central cabin would most likely be dead in the next twenty minutes, and what choice did Healy have?

All these years Healy had avoided performing any of the real Catholic rituals — communion and confession especially —

but now . . .

"It'd make me feel a lot better," the man said.

Healy glanced around the cabin. For the most part, the dying seemed to be over. That was how cholera generally worked. There was a siege and many died right away, and if you were lucky enough to survive the first siege then you had good chances of living.

There was sunlight now, and you could see on the faces of those lying on blankets across the cabin that their fevers had lessened somewhat and their knotting stomachs had calmed some and they did not call out for water quite so often.

Except for this man Hamilton.

He was in and out of consciousness — in and out of delirium, really — and you could see the color of his eyes fading.

He said now, "Please, Father. Hear my confession. I want to be ready."

Healy said, holding the man's hand, "I'm not really a priest, Hamilton. Not really."

But Hamilton grinned and said, "You're a good enough priest for the likes of me, Father."

So Healy heard Hamilton's confession and granted him absolution, and two minutes later there on the blanket, Hamilton died.

167

■ ■ ■ ■

Guild and James Bruckner reached the settlement early in the afternoon.

They went immediately to Kriker's cabin, and it was there they found the handcuffs.

They had been sawed in half and there was no sign whatsoever of Kriker.

They heard footsteps in the doorway, and there stood Father Healy.

In a quiet voice, he said, "I let him go, Mr. Guild. I let him go."

CHAPTER
TWENTY-ONE

Five minutes later, Guild, Bruckner, and Father Healy sat around the stove, sipping coffee and talking.

Healy said, "I owed him that, at least."

"Owed him what?" Guild said.

"One more chance at freedom. After all he did for those of us here in the settlement."

"You let an escaped murderer go."

"You much in the way of redemption, Mr. Guild?"

"Not a whole lot."

"I feel he's been redeemed."

"Half the killers in the Territory have got half the priests and ministers convinced of exactly that."

"And you don't believe them?"

"Not for a minute."

"You're mad, I take it?"

"You think I shouldn't be?"

"We're different people, Mr. Guild. My

feelings aren't yours." The priest smiled without any joy evident anywhere on his face. "Besides, you were the one who told me about comforting people."

"I don't see where that's got much to do with this."

"It's got everything to do with this, Mr. Guild."

"Like what?"

"His only solace will be in seeing the girl again. Alive and well. Then they'll have the chance to take off for California. He can live a good life there, Mr. Guild. I believe that sincerely."

Guild said to Bruckner, "You better pray your brother didn't hurt that girl." Guild sighed. He put his wet socks near the stove and said, "Christ."

"What?" said Bruckner.

"Now we've got to double back the way we came."

"What for?"

"Because that's where he'll go."

"Kriker?"

"Yeah."

Bruckner shook his head. "Sure hope he don't hurt Thomas."

Guild glanced at Healy and then at Bruckner. "Guess that's one thing I'll never understand."

"What's that?"

"After all the things your brother did to you, you still worry about him."

"He's my brother."

"He's also the man who threw kerosene on you and the man who sends you on every dirty job he needs doing."

"We all got our ways, Mr. Guild."

Guild sipped some more coffee and then glanced back at the priest. "How much of a head start he got on us?"

"Maybe an hour."

"Damn," Guild says. "He knows these hills a lot better than we do. He can beat us to the cabin."

Bruckner said, "There's a way through the pass."

"You know it?"

"I sort of know it."

Guild said, "That isn't exactly reassuring. You 'sort of' know it."

The man with the burned face looked as if he'd been slapped. "I'm tryin' to help, Mr. Guild."

Guild sighed. "Ah, Christ, kid," he said. "I know you are."

Then to the priest, Guild said, "Next time you want to let somebody go free, make sure it's somebody who doesn't know the mountains as well as Kriker does."

Then Guild and James Bruckner set off.

There had been no way to cut the cuffs themselves from his hands and ankles — only the chain that bound the cuffs together — so now as he pushed his calico through the heavy snow, Kriker's wrists sparkled in the afternoon sunlight. In the scabbard of the saddle rested the Sharps and in his holster sat a .44 of recent vintage.

All he could think of was the little girl. He saw her face that day of the robbery, when he'd taken her, and he saw her face all the times he tried to coax words from her, and he saw her face there at the last, on the cot when the cholera had come down on her.

Then he thought of California. He recalled a painting he'd seen of a bay up in the northern region, a beautiful schooner ship so elegant against the blue ocean sky, the trees in the surrounding cove impossibly lush and green. There was where the two of them belonged, he and his daughter. He would come to see her grow to womanhood and take a man worthy of her as a husband, and they would bear children and Kriker would finish his days with the gunfire of his early life faded in the distance of time, just an average citizen sitting in a rocker on a porch sweet with breezes and the tang of pipe smoke. He would be an old man in the best way to be an old man — at peace in his heart — and she would be a young woman in the best way to be a young woman — with peace in her heart and children like wild flowers dancing round her and a husband judge-sober and heart-peaceful as her companion and protector.

But then the sun angling off the snow blinded him and brought his mind back to the task at hand.

Without the money as trade, he would have to figure out how to get to the line shack and get the girl out without getting her killed.

He would kill Bruckner, of course.

About that there could be no doubt.

No doubt at all.

He rode on.

One of the posse men's horses stepped in a hole and snapped its leg twig-sharp.

The man put a gun to the horse's head and pulled the trigger twice.

The horse rolled over on its side and twitched only once, a great bloody shudder going through it there on the very white afternoon snow.

Then the man climbed on the back of another horse and the posse set off again.

Decker was still not saying much, his thoughts centered on the Bruckner brothers and how he had so smugly told the bounty man Guild that the Territory needed men like them. He had felt that he'd had the Bruckner brothers under control, that they might take the occasional bribe, that they might beat up the occasional whore after taking advantage of her services for free, but that they would not do anything so uncivic as to rob a bank or murder people.

He just hoped that the other young Territory lawmen who had taken those courses up in Yank-ton did not hear about all this. There would be a reunion of the men someday, and he did not want this tale told over tin buckets of beer, with the scorn of others who had taken the same courses but applied them with more success.

Decker dug his spurs into his mount.

James Bruckner turned out to be a better guide than Guild had figured. He took them up through steep pine, and he took them around a narrow treacherous ledge that saved them a long ride over a seemingly limitless stretch of plain, and he showed them how to cross a narrow stretch of river where the ice seemed to invite the laughter of children and the click of iron skates on the silver surface.

They stopped for a rest only once during the afternoon.

Guild watched Bruckner carefully. He could see that Bruckner had changed ever since the prospect of his brother being shot had become a distinct likelihood. He wondered if the man with the burned face might now try to make a break for it, get away and warn his brother somehow. It was a very long shot, James Bruckner being neither particularly intelligent nor particularly brave, but as the man went over by a naked black elm tree to put a yellow steaming stream into the snow, Guild kept his double 10-gauge pointed directly at the man's back. There had been a time when he had felt sorry for James Bruckner, and he supposed he still did. But this was before the little girl was taken. Now Guild did not care much at all about anything except getting her back safely.

Bruckner turned around and saw that the double 10-gauge was pointed directly at him.

"You gonna shoot me or somethin', Mr. Guild?"

Guild sighed, looking at the man's poor burned face. He lowered the gun and said, "Just get back up on your horse, Bruckner.

We've got to make better time than we have so far."

Bruckner had some difficulty getting mounted. Guild said, "Let's go."

Thomas Bruckner sat in the cabin knowing that something had gone wrong for sure.

By even the safest estimate, James should have been back with the money five hours ago.

But when he looked out the window, all Thomas Bruckner saw were the steep hills leading up to the cabin, and the timber to the north.

The timber would be a perfect place for a man to sneak up on the cabin and perhaps overwhelm the man inside. It would be much easier to fire from inside the timber than to fire from inside the cabin up to the timber.

Much easier.

He went back outside without being quite sure why. He stood under the cabin overhang and looked out at the vast white hills stretching before him. The late afternoon shadows were a soft blue. It was very beautiful and almost windless. The little wind there was whirled up snow like fine silt against his face, which reminded him of when he'd been a boy back on the farm and playing outdoors.

He wondered if James had gone and gotten himself killed. While James had become too much of a responsibility, and while Thomas had certainly planned to part company with his brother as soon as he got the money in hand, he did not want his brother to die, even if a part of him knew that James would probably be happier dead. Then no one could point to his face or snicker at it.

He went around the side of the cabin and checked on the little girl. She was still covered with enough snow that wandering animals would leave her alone. At least during the daylight hours. Night would be another matter. He considered the possibility of taking her inside tonight if James did not come back by then, but then he decided that would be just too eerie, sitting inside with a little dead girl wrapped in the blanket. He hoped for her sake the animals did not get her, but he guessed in the long run it didn't matter much at all. He did not like to think of himself as mean, but he was adamant about thinking of himself as practical.

He went back and stood under the overhang and let the fine cold silty snow cover his face and make his cheeks rosy and make him feel wide awake. He wished he had some good whiskey and a good woman, and he wished he had the bank money. He wished he'd had a clean friendly parting with his brother, and he wished he were on a transcontinental train, one where black porters waited on your every whim, and where you could sit in a private room and look out at the rolling plains and smoke a cigar and have not a worry about anything at all.

He was wishing for all these things when the first bullet sliced into the frame of the door next to him.

CHAPTER
TWENTY-TWO

There were some small granite hills that provided a windbreak. Guild stopped to talk, since the horses needed a rest.

"You're going down to that cabin and you're going to tell your brother that he won't get out alive unless he hands the girl over. You understand?"

James Bruckner gulped. "Yessir."

"Then you're going to bring the girl straight up here, and then I'm going to go in and take your brother just as peaceful as he'll let me. You understand?"

"Yessir."

"That is, if Kriker doesn't kill him first."

"Oh, Jesus."

Guild saw how scared he'd made James Bruckner. "I didn't say Kriker would do that. I only said it was a possibility."

"Yessir."

Night was black in the sky and blue on the ground. The granite cliffs were without

179

detail now, just looming black shapes. The horses shit steaming sweet road apples. Guild pulled on beef jerky. Bruckner, too upset, declined to join them.

Guild said, "You going to do exactly what I say, James?"

"Yes."

"Your brother's going to hang. You know that, don't you?"

"Yessir."

"I'll testify in your behalf. I think I can convince the judge that you didn't kill Rig or Tolliver."

"I don't want him to die, Mr. Guild. He's taken care of me all my life. He really has."

"He hasn't done a real good job of it, son."

"He's not a bad man, sir. Not a real bad one. Just sort of — rambunctious. That's what Pa always called him. Rambunctious."

"How many men you suppose he's killed?"

"None he didn't have to."

"I see," Guild said. He swung back up on his horse. The wind was coming up. Guild thought of Rig and young Tolliver and how Thomas Bruckner had killed them so effortlessly. "Rambunctious, huh?" he said to James Bruckner. "Rambunctious."

They set off again. The night, despite its beauty, was starting to get bitter.

CHAPTER
TWENTY-THREE

He knew many things about the pine trees, Kriker did. He knew the white pine and the jack pine and the bristlecone pine and the ponderosa pine. He knew that some pine needles were soft and could be used as mattresses when you were camping out, and he knew that some pine needles were hard and could be used in making roofs. He liked the clean sweet high perfume of pines, especially at cold dusk such as now, and he knew few sights so beautiful as a sloping valley of pines, green tops vivid against a pure white sweep of snow beneath. He had lived in these hills four decades now, and the sight of pines — like a cub bear or pink squirming infant born to a settlement woman — still had the power to move him deeply.

But for now such thoughts were beyond Kriker as he positioned himself behind an especially wide pine trunk and looked down the hill at the line shack where Thomas

Bruckner held the girl.

Next to Kriker were two large canvas sacks weighted down with rocks. They would suffice from a distance to convince Bruckner that Kriker had the money and was willing to make the trade.

Dusk was now a deep purple. Stars stretched from horizon to horizon, sharp and brilliant against the streaked dark sky. The moon was full and silver.

Kriker, hefting his rifle, walked up to the edge of the clearing and shouted down to the cabin. He let go two shots.

"Bruckner! Can you hear me!" he shouted.

He knew it would be awhile before Bruckner responded.

Bruckner knew the voice at once. The whiskey and tobacco rasp of it was unmistakable even from this distance. All he could wonder was what Kriker himself was doing here. Where was James? Where was the money?

Then the worst realization of all struck him.

He had been going to carry the dead body of the girl to a point near the settlement, then drop her off in exchange for the money. By the time they learned the girl was dead, he and James would be gone.

But now —

Being on the side of the law, being the pursuer instead of the pursued, had kept Thomas Bruckner unfamiliar with panic. The authority of the law was very good for steadying your nerves.

But out here — the wilderness at night — the authority of the law did not matter.

Especially when a man such as Kriker — a man who'd vaguely frightened Thomas Bruckner even when they'd been working together — obviously meant to kill him.

Kriker shouted, "I have the money with me, Bruckner! I want the girl!"

In the endless blue-shadowed night, Kriker's voice was as imposing as an Old Testament prophet's.

The next time Kriker shouted, "I want the girl!" Thomas Bruckner had the clear impression that the man had crept much closer to the cabin.

Beneath his heavy clothing, Bruckner's body was soaked with sweat. His eyes scanned the pines and the foothills beneath but found no sign of Kriker.

Given the mountain man's ability to track and hunt, he could be anywhere.

Kriker swung wide east, in an arc that took

him down a deep valley and back up a hill slick with ice. He had to lift his feet high and bring them down heavily for purchase. Then another deep valley and another ice-slick rise awaited him. His intent was to come up from behind the cabin. He was panting and short of breath when he reached the top of the second rise. The satchels of rocks were thrown over his shoulder. His rifle dangled from his right hand. He was thinking about the time he'd brought the girl the store-bought shoes and how he'd had to put them on her himself and how for the first time she'd smiled on that sunny May morning.

Sheriff Decker and the posse reached the settlement just at the time when Father Healy and the granny woman were trying to help the people who'd survived the cholera go back to their cabins and take up their normal lives. There would be long days of nourishment no more substantial than beef broth, and there would be long nights of faint but not fatal nausea, and there would be the grief resulting from the deaths of seventeen people they'd known as friends and neighbors here in the settlement.

The posse came down the hill, their horses kicking up a dust storm of snow in the silver moonlight.

When they came into the settlement proper, they smelled of hard riding and the cold. Their mounts smelled of heat and manure.

Sheriff Decker found Father Healy waiting for him in front of the main cabin.

For most of his life, having grown up scruffy on the streets of Chicago, Healy had always feared lawmen of any sort. Now he found himself facing Decker with a certain self-confidence. He was not sure why, but when he nodded and introduced himself as "Father Healy," he felt for the first time as if this were a fact — he really was a priest now — and not merely a ruse to hide behind.

"I want the Bruckner brothers," Decker said. He sounded exhausted.

"We were just preparing a meal. Why don't you join us?"

Decker glanced back at the men behind him. It had been a hard, fast ride. A break would probably be good for them.

He nodded and let the priest lead him and the others inside the cabin where, five minutes later, the granny woman ladled out beef broth. She also handed out big chunks of fresh wheat bread.

Sheriff Decker was a dunker. He dunked

his bread so deep and so long in his soup he could scarcely lift the bread up again. Yet he managed to do so each time. As he dunked and ate, he said, "I want the Bruckners and I want Kriker."

"Kriker is gone, too."

"The girl who rode in told me that the bounty man had Kriker handcuffed and under arrest. How'd he get away?"

Some of Father Healy's old fear of lawmen returned. He could not bring himself to tell Decker that he had let Kriker go. "He just got away."

"I assume he went to the line shack to find the little girl?"

"I assume."

"You don't sound disturbed by that?"

"By what?"

"By a man like Kriker getting away."

"Kriker's a very complicated man."

"He's a killer."

"He didn't kill Rig or Tolliver."

"Maybe not," Decker said. "But he's killed other people."

"The girl has changed him. She's made him gentle."

"Is that why he robbed the bank? Because he's so gentle? Is that why he escaped?"

"There are different ways of being gentle."

"If you know anything about him that can

help me, Father, I'd appreciate it if you'd tell me."

The priest shrugged. "I know what you know. Nothing more."

Decker fixed him with a cynical eye. "I have a cousin who's a priest."

"I see."

"He was ordained in St. Louis. Bishop Morgan ordained him."

"Ah, Bishop Morgan."

"Who ordained you, Father?"

He knew there was panic in his face, and then a rush of blood from embarrassment. In his way Decker was a subtle and devious man. Healy stammered, "Bishop Wright."

"Bishop Wright? I don't believe I've ever heard of him."

"Chicago."

"Bishop O'Keefe is in Chicago."

"Bishop Wright served before Bishop O'Keefe."

Decker's eyes had not left Healy's. Something like a smirk was beginning to tug on his lips. "Bishop Wright. I see."

A tall woman in soiled clothes appeared in the doorway. She seemed intimidated by the posse. But she drew herself up and came over to Healy and Decker.

"Hello, Mary," the priest said.

Then the woman smiled. "She's fine now,

187

Father. Our daughter."

"I'm happy for you, Mary." He took her hand and held it gently.

"It was your prayin', Father. It was your prayin'."

"No, Mary, it was God's will."

"I just wanted to thank you, Father."

Father Healy smiled. "Thank God, Mary. He's the one who should be thanked."

She leaned over and gave him a tender kiss on the forehead, all the more tender for the roughness of her life and manner. "We all want you to know how much we appreciate what you done for us, Father."

Then she left.

When he turned back around to look at Decker, he saw something peculiar had happened to the sheriff's hard flat gaze. It had softened considerably.

Decker said, "They seem to appreciate you here."

"They're very kind people, really."

"I've often been told that a lot of them have criminal pasts." He did not say this nearly as harshly as he might have.

"People change, Sheriff."

Decker stared at the empty doorway through which Mary had just come and gone. "They're raising families now, eh?"

"Yes."

188

"And working the land?"

"Yes."

Decker paused now. "And obeying the law now, Father?"

"Oh, definitely," Father Healy said. "Definitely obeying the law."

Decker stood up and pushed out his hand. "Bishop Wright must train his priests well. You did a good job with the cholera outbreak."

"Thank you."

Decker tugged on his hat. His brown eyes were a lawman's eyes again. "I'm going to have to take them all in, Father. The Bruckners and Kriker."

"You'll bring the little girl back here?"

Decker stared at him a moment. "Is she kin of someone here?"

Father Healy smiled. He seemed both proud and sad at the same time. "That's the nice thing about this settlement, Sheriff."

"What's that?"

"We're all kin here. Just the way God planned for us."

Decker shrugged into his sheepskin coat and put out his hand and shook with the priest. "You give my best to Bishop Wright."

Their eyes held on each other steadily.

"Yes," Father Healy said. "Yes, I'll be sure

to do that."

Warmed now, and ready again for the last and most dangerous part of their trek, the posse went outdoors and mounted up.

The horses streamed silver from their nostrils, and the night seemed vast with brilliant yellow stars and the far lonely cry of a barn owl.

Father Healy stood watching the men depart. Then he surprised himself by doing something he had never been able to before. He said a prayer. It was a ragged and informal prayer and not at all the sort of thing a true church man would pray. But it was a prayer, and it did imply, however fragilely, that he had come to believe in some power larger than man's. If not God then some sort of hope that made the night less dark. Perhaps it would be all he would ever have and enough at that.

He was praying for Harry Kriker.

CHAPTER
TWENTY-FOUR

Thomas Bruckner opened the cabin door and shouted out, "I want you to listen to something, Kriker."

His voice echoed in the deep blue shadows of the winter night.

"I want you to listen to how you're going to get the girl back."

He could hear a distant coyote. He could hear a distant moose. He could hear a distant dog. But in the stillness that lay thick as snow on the hills surrounding the cabin, he could not hear Harry Kriker.

"I'm going to walk the girl and my horse down the hill a ways. Then I'm going to walk the girl back to the cabin. While I'm in the cabin, I want you to put the money on my horse. Then I'll mount up and leave the girl about a mile away. You understand?"

But there was just the silence of the vast blue night again. Just the silence.

Thomas Bruckner had the terrible feeling

that somehow Kriker knew the girl was dead and was now merely closing in.

But no.

There was no way that could have happened.

Bruckner went back inside the cabin. He worked quickly. He took a blanket and bundled soft pillows inside it until it looked to be about the size the girl would be, and then he took his carbine and went outside to his horse. Ice had formed on the animal's nostrils. Bruckner chipped it away with the edge of his hand.

Then he mounted up. He was careful with the blanket that was supposed to be the girl. If Kriker was watching — as was very likely — then he would expect Bruckner to be careful with the bundle.

Bruckner rode down the hill. Twice the horse got scared, slipping on ice. Its teeth gnashed and it made a moaning sound. Bruckner made a very similar sound. He wanted it to be over. He knew how crazy a man Kriker was. He'd always known.

He led the horse down to a flat next to a twisted oak tree. It wasn't quite an eighth of a mile from the cabin. The moonlight on the ice around the tree was silver. Silty snow made Bruckner's face red and cold again. He ground-tied the horse, then hefted the bundle that was supposed to be the girl and he put his Colt tight against where the girl's head would be in the bundle. He just assumed Kriker was watching. From somewhere. Nobody knew how to hide — even in snow — as well as a man raised in the mountains.

He kept the gun pointed good and direct and hard at the head of the bundle, and then he started making his way back to the cabin.

Wind came and with it dust devils again, white and whirling across the blue shadows on the snow. There was no sound except the wind. He smelled his own sweat and felt how badly he needed a shave and felt suddenly an almost violent need to take a leak, and he thought of his brother and of how he should not treat him the way he sometimes did.

But mostly he thought of Kriker. Where he could be. What he planned to do.

When Bruckner finally pushed open the door to the cabin, he found out what he'd been wondering about.

Just what he'd been wondering about.

Kriker stepped from behind the door and jammed the barrel of his rifle right into the back of Bruckner's head.

Bruckner dropped his Colt to the floor. It

sounded very loud dropping just there just then.

Kriker said, "Now you put that little girl down real easy on that cot over there. Then you and me are going to have us a talk."

Thomas Bruckner did not get frightened or angry or sad. He simply sighed, sighed and walked with his Texas boots loud against the wooden floor across the cabin and laid down his bundle on the cot.

"Now," Kriker said, "get her unbundled so I can get a look at her."

"Jesus," Thomas Bruckner said to himself. "Jesus." It was as much a prayer as a curse.

He leaned down and unbundled the girl.

Then he paused.

"I said get her unbundled," Kriker said.

But a curious paralysis had come over Thomas Bruckner. He felt like the time his father had caught him stealing change from his father's overall trousers in the closet. His father had said, "Thomas William, why do you have your hand in my pocket?" "I don't know." "You don't know why you have your hand in my pocket?" "No, Pa, I don't." "Well, Thomas, you're not only a thief, you're a liar." Then his father had really given it to him and given it to him good.

Only this was going to be worse.

Much, much worse.

"You unbundle her so I can look at her," Kriker said. But he had started to sound suspicious.

"I can't," Thomas Bruckner said.

"Why not?"

"Because she ain't."

"She ain't what?"

"She ain't in there."

There was a terrible silence. "She ain't in there?"

"No, she ain't."

"Where is she then?"

"She's . . ."

"She's where?"

"She's . . ."

"Where?"

"Outside."

"Outside?"

"Harry, I didn't do nothin' to her."

"Jesus Christ, you sonofabitch."

Bruckner could feel Harry Kriker ready to go. He had been violated in the worst way possible, and when he let himself go it was going to be just unimaginable.

But Kriker surprised Thomas Bruckner by saying, "She's out in the snow?"

"I didn't want her to smell."

Kriker didn't say anything.

"It was the cholera, Harry. I didn't do nothin' to her. You know I wouldn't do nothin' to a little kid like that, Harry."

Kriker still didn't say anything.

"I got her back here and I laid her out on the cot and I put a couple of good warm blankets over her and I gave her water and I asked her if she needed anything. I kept her just as comfortable as I could, and then she just . . ."

Kriker pulled back the hammer on his rifle.

"Then she just . . ." Thomas Bruckner said.

He didn't need to finish his sentence, and he didn't in fact finish his sentence.

In a voice quieter than Bruckner could ever have imagined, Harry Kriker said, "She speak?"

"What?"

"She talk to you?"

"No."

"Not a word?"

"No."

"Not no kind of sound at all?"

"Not no kind of sound."

Kriker pulled the trigger four times. The first bullet tore away Thomas Bruckner's nose and part of his forehead; the second bullet took away his jaw; the third bullet tore a big red hole in his neck, and the fourth bullet made a soft explosion of

Thomas Bruckner's chest from a side angle.

There was a great deal of noise and a great deal of smoke. Then there was just the silence again.

After a time of just standing there and looking down at Thomas Bruckner's body, Kriker went outside the cabin into the chill night. He wanted to find the girl, and it did not take him long at all to find her. It was obvious by the mound of snow to the east of the cabin.

He got down on his hands and knees and scooped her out. It took ten minutes.

She was already discolored, and she was already frozen solid.

He knelt there and stared at her.

He wished she'd talked to him, said just one word, at least once.

He wondered what that word would have been.

And then it fell over him, an animal grief that took the form of a kind of baying sound and a shuddering accompanied by soft silent tears as his rough hands traced the cold lines of her tiny beautiful face.

He wanted to cry and needed to cry, but he could not cry. There were just those few tears. All he could do was kneel beside her body and make that baying sound and rock back and forth as if the swaying relieved the grief that gripped him.

He just wished that she had uttered a single word to him in their years together.

He just wished he knew what that word would have been.

He was wondering about this when he heard the horses on the rise to the west.

He turned and saw two riders silhouetted against the moon and the ink-blue sky.

CHAPTER
TWENTY-FIVE

Guild said, "You want to call out to him?"

"Thomas?"

"Yeah."

"Okay."

"I don't want him taking any shots at me. I want you to tell him I've got a gun on you and I plan to use it."

"Thomas won't want me to die."

"Good," Guild said. "Then I won't have to kill you." He was tired and he was cold. In weather like this it was easy for the infirmities of age to begin their tireless work on you, sinus trouble in the nose and constipation in the bowels. He wanted in this wind and this night to get the little girl and the robbery money and take them back to their rightful places.

As they came down the hill, the deep shadows of the trees playing gamely across the blue snow, Guild said, "Call out."

Still shackled to the saddlehorn, James

Bruckner couldn't cup his hands to shout, so he merely threw back his head and began bellowing.

"You don't shoot now, hear, Thomas? 'Cause Mr. Guild's got a gun on me. Hear?"

Even in the gloom Guild could see his burned face. The poor bastard, Guild thought. Even in the shadows he didn't look like other people.

They made earnest progress through the deep snow, the horses tiring easily, and as they drew even closer, Guild said again, "Call out one more time."

"Wind takes your voice right away, don't it?" James Bruckner said.

Guild nodded for him to yell again.

They were maybe thirty yards away from the cabin when the door burst open, and silhouetted there in the lamplight was the unmistakable form of Harry Kriker.

He had his rifle, and he said only one thing: "You and your brother killed the little girl!"

"Killed her?" James Bruckner started to say.

But Kriker didn't give him any time, no time at all.

Kriker charged through the snow right toward the horses, and he shot James Bruckner clean in the face.

Bruckner's body wanted to fall off the saddle, but the cuffs kept him hanging there.

Kriker went over and started kicking Bruckner in the ribs.

Guild came around the horse and brought the butt of his rifle down hard on the back of Kriker's head.

He was amazed that the blow merely staggered Kriker, didn't knock him out at all.

Kriker spun, his rifle ready.

"They killed the girl."

"I'm sorry, Kriker."

"They took the girl and they killed her."

He was shouting, he was crying, he was crazy. He pumped another bullet into the dead man.

"He's dead already, Kriker."

Kriker sobbed, then turned back to Guild.

"They killed the girl," he said.

"I doubt they meant to. They didn't seem the kind. Not really."

Kriker's eyes were something Guild could not bear to see.

"You defendin' them?"

"No. I'm just sayin' it was probably an accident is all." He paused. "You'll have to go back along with the money."

"What?" Kriker said.

"I'm afraid so."

Kriker cocked the rifle. "You try to take

me in, bounty man, and we're both gonna die. Right here and right now."

"I don't want to have to kill you," Guild said.

"You can't kill me."

"You haven't been keeping track of your bullets."

"The hell."

"You haven't."

"I got two rounds left."

"You got no rounds left."

Kriker hesitated just long enough for Guild to raise the butt of his rifle and bring it down again on the side of Kriker's face.

This time Guild got a pure clean shot at Kriker's temple, and that made a good deal of difference.

Kriker collapsed on the ground.

Guild took the horses around the back of the cabin where they'd be out of the woods, and then he went to the side of the cabin and looked at the dead girl, and then he dragged Kriker inside the cabin. He had taken his last pair of handcuffs from his saddlebag. He cuffed Kriker to the chair. Guild figured Decker and his men would soon be here.

Kriker came awake ten minutes later. Blood was matted in his hair. He looked like an old animal that was dying out his time in confusion and some inexplicable despair.

They sat in the cabin and Guild read a Yankton newspaper from three years ago detailing the Territory's plans to start a mandatory educational system, an idea that was not meeting with a great deal of favor.

Kriker said, "I want to go see the girl."

A thin wind came up, swirling the snow like topsoil. The wind was musical. In Indian legend it was said that this particular kind of music could only be heard over cursed soil or death ground. Given all the people who had died in the past two days, the notion seemed to have a particular relevance.

"I want to go see her."

"Wouldn't be a good idea."

"I don't give a damn she's dead, Guild. I just want to see her."

Guild sighed and put down his paper. "You believe in God?"

"No."

"Then I can't help you much, I guess."

"You gonna tell me about the angels?"

"I was gonna tell you to calm down."

"You don't know how much I loved her."

"I think I can guess."

"I just want to go see her."

"I just want you to stay put."

He started crying then, and Guild had to look away. The sound Kriker made was harsh, and Guild would remember it for a long time.

"You really gonna take me in?"

"I got to, Kriker."

"They'll just hang me."

"That isn't up to me."

"I didn't kill Rig or Tolliver."

"No, but you killed other people before."

"I don't want to die that way."

"What way?"

"In public and all. Them ladies in their fancy hats standin' down there and glarin' up at you."

"I don't have any choice, Kriker."

"You could let me go."

"No."

"You could say I escaped."

"No."

He didn't say anything then for a long time, and Guild rattled the newspaper back into reading shape and put an unlit cigar in his mouth and went back to reading.

Kriker said, "I got a Colt inside my sheepskin pocket. Belonged to Thomas Bruckner."

Guild put down the paper, curious. "Why would you tell me that? Why wouldn't you try to use it to escape?"

"Because I don't want to escape."

"You want me to take the gun?"

"No, not that either."

"Then what?"

Kriker sighed. "Some ways, we're alike."

"I suspect that's true."

"You had some learnin', didn't you?"

"Some. Not a lot."

"You speak fine."

"Worked for a marshal once who was real high on books."

"He real high on dignity?"

"Meaning?"

"Meaning them ladies in their fancy hats lookin' up at you."

Guild was just starting to catch on. He did not feel so bright. It had taken him a long and laborious time to catch on.

Just at dawn Guild went outside the cabin and peed in the snow. There was just enough light that the urine was yellow in the white snow.

The shot came just after.

CHAPTER TWENTY-SIX

Guild went in and took the cuffs off Kriker, and then he heaved Kriker up on his shoulders and carried him outside and laid him out next to the girl. In the morning now you could hear dogs and you could hear distant bawling cattle.

Kriker had done a good clean job of it. There was a hole, a messy one, in the back of his head. Guild wondered if he had been afraid. Guild would have been afraid.

Without quite knowing why, Guild knelt down next to Kriker and took the dead man's hand and placed it over the heart of the little girl.

Then he started digging snow up with both his hands, and he covered them good, the two of them, and then he stood up and looked out on the unfurling white land. There was blue sky and a full yellow sun. Warmer now, there was even that kind of sweetness that comes on sunny winter days.

It made him think of pretty women on ice skates, their cheeks touched perfect red by the cold, their eyes daring and blue.

He did not look back at Kriker and the girl. They were done, and Guild had enough ghosts inside him. He did not need more.

He had to pee again — he always got this way after terrible things — and then he went to his saddlebags and got some jerky and then he went inside and picked up the paper again and finally lit up the cigar.

Decker and his men came and, of course being parents themselves, made much of the little girl. One man got sick and one man started to cry.

What Decker mostly wanted to know about, standing there inside the cabin with Guild, was how something like this could have happened.

"How the hell'd he get a gun and kill himself that way?"

All Guild said was, "Damned if I know."

Ten minutes later they packed the little girl across the rump of one horse and Kriker across the rump of another, and then they set out the long white distance back to the town.

CHAPTER
TWENTY-SEVEN

When they got in, Decker told Guild to come around in the morning for the reward money. He still did not sound happy that the town had been cheated out of a hanging. In Yankton, Guild thought, in those law courses Decker had taken, they'd probably taught him that folks just naturally liked a hanging every now and then, and here Guild had gone and robbed him of it.

Guild went over to the house he'd been at the other night. He asked for the straw-haired girl. She came out from behind the blue chenille curtains downstairs wearing the same gingham dress and the shoes one size too big. The way they forced her to walk, with sort of a girlish but fetching lack of grace, made him think she was even more of a kid than she was.

The madam put a hand on Guild's arm and led him off to the side. She was a skinny woman who wore hard pink mascara like a death mask. "She ain't real reliable, truth to tell." She nodded to a woman who looked much as the madam must have looked twenty years earlier. "Whyn't you taken Aberdeen over there?"

Guild shrugged. "Straw-haired one's fine."

Upstairs he said, "Mind if I blow out that kerosene lamp?"

"I done it twice last night, but I don't feel like doin' it tonight. That's why Patty's so mad at me."

"You didn't answer my question."

"About the lamp?"

"About the lamp."

"I don't care if you blow it out."

So he blew it out and then he went over and sat in the rocking chair that faced the street below. You could see stars, and closer to the glass of the window you could see snow. The wind came in torrents and the glass rattled, and through the cracks you could feel cold. There was laughter in the next room but it sounded sad.

He said, "Would you sit on my lap?"

She said, "Mister, you really should've taken Aberdeen."

"You ever answer a question directly?"

"I sit on your lap?"

"Yes."

"That's all you want me to do?"

"Yes."

"I won't charge you, then."

"One other thing, too."

"I figured."

"Don't talk."

"What?"

"Don't say anything. Just sit on my lap and don't say anything. Don't say anything at all."

"Okay." For the first time, she sounded hesitant, maybe even a little afraid.

But she came over and sat on his lap. Guild kept his word. He did not touch her. He just let her sit there on his knee the way he'd once held a daughter and sometimes a wife. That had been long, long ago. Sitting there in the darkness he thought again of the little girl he'd killed that time, and then he thought of the little girl who'd died of cholera. He thought of James Bruckner's burned face, and he thought of the way the bullet had sounded, so sharp, the one from Kriker's gun when Kriker'd put the Colt in his mouth and pulled the trigger.

Then the wind came again and the window shook and he could feel the cold clean draft.

He sighed, and it was a very deep sigh,

and she said, there in the darkness with her perfume and her sweet farm-girl face, "You all right, mister?"

And he sighed again and just stared out the window at the distant meaningless stars and said, "No, I don't suppose I am."

To that, she said nothing at all.

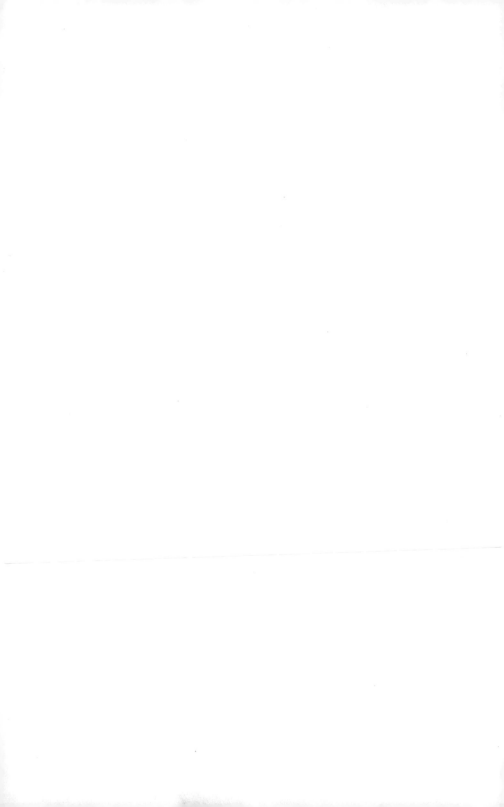